MW01602188

ROSEBUD HOPES

JULIA CLEMENS

PICKLED PLUM PUBLISHING

Copyright © 2022 by Julia Clemens

All rights reserved.

No part of this book may be reproduced in any form or by any electronic or mechanical means, including information storage and retrieval systems, without written permission from the author, except for the use of brief quotations in a book review.

For Kanani, Taryn, Amber, Kiana, Steph, Andrea, Carli and all of my high school homies. I doubt we would have survived running an inn together but we would have had a blast trying!

CHAPTER ONE

"I THINK God might have accidentally sent angels when he gifted you with those sons of yours." Emmie, the nurse who had been overseeing Hazel's chemo treatment that day, smiled as she unhooked Hazel from her very last IV.

Hazel returned the smile, feeling exhausted but victorious. She was done. Chemo was now part of her past, and she prayed it would stay that way. Her future held many doctor's visits before she could truly be considered in remission, but she'd completed the allotted rounds of chemo treatments—all five horrifying months of them—and she wasn't looking back.

The cute, young nurse had been on the receiving end of a number of meaningful glances from each of Hazel's teenaged sons, so it was gracious of her to see past that—to notice the two young men who'd sat by their mother for the past three hours as she fought through this last treatment.

"I think you're the angel, Emmie," ventured Chase, Hazel's older son, as he stood from his seat and slid his phone into his back pocket.

Hazel fought the urge to roll her eyes at her son's blatant flirting. Emmie was young, but not young enough for her still-in-high-school son. Yes, he'd be graduating in the next month, but Emmie had to be in her early, or maybe even mid, twenties.

"I'll let my husband and daughter know you think so," Emmie replied, her eyes dancing.

Sterling, Hazel's younger son, burst into laughter as Chase's face burned a bright red.

"But thank you for the sentiment, Chase," Emmie continued as she gathered up the last of her supplies and turned her attention to Hazel. "I'll be back for you all in a few minutes." She winked at Hazel before leaving the room.

Hazel was exhausted—this final round of chemo had really kicked her behind. But at the same time she felt her spirits rise. She was done. She'd fought cancer. She still wasn't sure if she'd won or not, but the fact that she'd withstood the poison even now swirling through her veins was a victory.

As Emmie left, Hazel's head turned toward her boys. Sterling was still laughing as Chase slumped in his seat.

"Shut up," Chase muttered to Sterling.

"But that was brutal," Sterling snickered, slapping his knee.

"Hey, at least I was man enough to shoot my shot. You thought she was just as pretty as I did, but you just sat there."

"And watched you get re-jec-ted," Sterling teased.

Chase glared but then glanced toward his mom, knowing she wouldn't appreciate their fighting.

"Sorry for hitting on your nurse, Mom." Chase really was acting the part of the angel Emmie had pegged him to be. A few years ago he couldn't have cared less if he'd stepped on his mom's toes, but this Chase was a mature version of the one who'd left Rosebud angry and hating the world. He'd come back to town with his dad when Hazel had been diagnosed with breast cancer and his attitude had done a one-eighty. Not only that, but her relationship with her son was now more solid than it had ever been. Hazel still hated cancer, but she did have to give it this one small credit.

"And sorry for fighting," Sterling added, either not wanting to be outdone by his brother or truly feeling remorse.

Judging by his crestfallen look and the abrupt cessation of laughter, Hazel was going with the latter.

"Don't worry about it. That was actually highly entertaining, Chase. I don't know that I've ever seen you in action," she joked.

Chase shot Hazel a smirk that all the girls at school found devastating, according to him. "That was nothing, Mom. You should see me when I'm trying. I totally knew Emmie was too old for me but wanted to give her ego a little boost, ya know?"

"Whatever," Sterling muttered. Clearly the smirk didn't have an effect on him.

Chase didn't respond to his annoyed little brother but instead focused his attention to his mom.

"Was it just as bad as all the others?" he asked, nodding toward the now-bandaged arm where the IV had fed that horrid iciness into her veins.

"Maybe the worst yet. But somehow the best at the same time," Hazel responded, trying to sound light even though all she wanted was a nap.

Her boys nodded in understanding. Hazel had already explained that after the third month of chemo, although each round became continuously harder on her body, just knowing that she had passed the halfway point had been the lift her spirit had needed at the time. And each subsequent treatment meant she was closer to the end, so even as her body could barely carry itself, her spirit was jubilant.

"I'll go find a wheelchair," Sterling offered, folding the chessboard he'd brought to occupy his time.

"It's okay," Hazel said. "I'm pretty sure Emmie will bring one back with her."

Sterling dropped back into his seat with a gloating look at his brother. Chase carefully ignored it, but the very tops of his cheeks had a reddish tint.

Hazel watched as Chase warred with the temptation to retaliate but chose not to. Sterling started to taunt his brother but then looked toward his mom and closed his mouth instead, knowing Hazel would want them to keep the peace.

Both boys had insisted on coming with Hazel to support her in her last treatment, although it would be a boring three hours of watching their mother being pumped full of the substance that could save her but that was also slowly killing off parts of her. It wasn't exactly where any teenaged boy would want to be, and not where Hazel wanted them either. They'd asked to come before and each time Hazel had put them off. But this time Chase and Sterling had insisted on staying at her side from beginning to end. Of course they'd often come along for pick-up or drop-off with her parents, or sometimes Dylan or Wells, her kind-of boyfriend and ex-husband (long story), but this was the first time both boys had come together and sat through the whole thing with her. And for that Hazel wasn't just grateful, she was proud.

They'd each brought something to entertain themselves during the long hours: Chase his phone and charger and Sterling his chessboard and a book. If those choices didn't show her boys' personalities, Hazel had no idea what would.

Hazel tugged the blanket she'd brought from home more tightly around her body and tried not to shiver. The hospital room where she received treatments was warmer than others she'd been in, both temperature-wise and in décor. The walls were a soft cream instead of stark white and there were framed photos of picturesque travel sites. She knew they also cranked the heat up because of how the process of chemo could chill the body. It was so warm in her room that both boys had taken off their hats and were probably still sweating in their t-shirts and shorts. But neither had complained once.

Emmie was right. They really were angels.

"Knock, knock." Hazel heard her mother's voice from the other side of the door.

"Come in," Sterling offered.

As the door opened, Hazel saw not only her parents, but Dylan and Wells too.

"Wow," was all she could manage as she dropped her head onto the pillows behind her. She was incredibly grateful for the support, but she was also unbelievably exhausted. The only thing that kept her going was the knowledge of what was coming next, the action she'd earned the right to do. The reason everyone was here with her.

"Tough one?" asked Robert, Hazel's dad.

Hazel assumed one of her boys nodded, but since she'd now closed her eyes she couldn't see what was happening in the room. She wanted to interact with her family, but she couldn't seem to raise her heavy eyelids.

Hazel heard someone sit beside her and a hand take hers. Judging by how small the hand was, she knew it was her mother. Well, that and she could smell her mother's signature gardenia scent, which she'd worn for as long as Hazel could remember. Thankfully the smell didn't nauseate her the way so many others did. After some chemo treatments Hazel had had to beg her dad to roll down the windows because the gardenia smell was too strong, but her stomach seemed to be cooperating better today and, as she thought about it, the smell was lighter. She wondered if her mom had refrained from applying any that morning and this was just her residual scent. Hazel sent up another prayer of gratitude that even though she was enduring medical horror, at least she was facing it with the very best people on the planet.

Speaking of which . . . where were the girls? She doubted her friends would let this day come and go without being here for her.

Hazel managed to lift her eyelids and saw six pairs of eyes staring back at her. Had they just spent the last couple of minutes watching her? She realized she hadn't heard any conversation so it did make sense. That was somehow creepy and sweet at the same time.

Hazel was just about to ask where her friends were when there was another quick knock at the door. Emmie had reappeared with a wheelchair in tow.

Hazel's family moved out of the way, and Chase edged awkwardly behind Sterling, avoiding Emmie's line of sight as she came to Hazel's side.

"Are you ready for this?" Emmie asked with a bright smile.

"I've only been dreaming of this day for the past five months." Hazel somehow managed to return Emmie's grin despite her exhaustion.

"Then let's do this." Somehow Emmie's small frame managed to heave Hazel into the chair with an ease and gentleness that seemed impossible. Nurses really were their own brand of superhero.

After arranging Hazel in the chair, Emmie stepped back and Hazel's boys seemed to understand it was now their turn. They took their positions on either side of Hazel's chair, Sterling maneuvering the left handle and Chase the right as they pushed Hazel to the doorway. Judging by the number of footsteps she heard behind her, Hazel knew the rest of her family was following.

As Hazel emerged from her room, she saw the hall lined with people. Amy, the nurse who had comforted Hazel as she'd first experienced chemo, helping her find the strength to over-come her petrifying fear, was clapping wildly, her red curls dancing on her shoulders. Dr. Hansen stood next to Amy with a wide smile on his face, his claps a little more subdued but just as heartfelt.

Hazel took in face after face, the people who had buoyed her up, silently or not so silently cheering her on through her journey. They were all here, along with a few Hazel didn't know but who were cheering just as hard. They all knew and understood what Hazel had overcome, and because of that they were celebrating.

But it was the face on her level that made Hazel pause. A girl hunched in a wheelchair beside Amy, looking every bit as exhausted as Hazel. Her eyes were filled with wariness as she watched Hazel riding down that hall.

Hazel understood that wariness. She'd felt it when she'd watched others "graduate" from chemo as well. When she had been in the thick of it she couldn't imagine this day ever coming, even though she'd dreamed about it constantly. She knew why that young girl was there. Many of the staff felt it was good for those in the middle of chemo to celebrate with those who were done—to give them hope in the visual reminder that they too would be done someday.

And for the most part Hazel had felt hopeful through the three graduations she'd witnessed. But a tiny bit of her hadn't fully believed she'd ever be on this side of it. She wanted to be sure this young woman didn't hold that same doubt.

She reached back to touch Chase's hand and he stopped quickly. Sterling took another step before he realized what was happening, which actually worked out perfectly to angle her toward the young woman. They sat facing each other, nearly knee to knee.

"How long?" Hazel asked. She didn't have many words left

in her, at least not until after she took a long, long nap. But she needed to connect with this girl, even if it took the rest of her strength.

"Two months down, one to go," the girl responded in a thin voice.

Hazel smiled. She hoped the mere three months of treatment meant the girl's cancer hadn't progressed too far before they'd caught it. That she had a better chance than most at beating this. And yet Hazel knew that in that moment it probably didn't matter much to her. What mattered was that she was in chemo, having her body cleansed while also being polluted, and she still had a month of misery left.

"You've got this," Hazel said, meeting the girl's eyes.

The girl pursed her lips but then began nodding even as her eyes filled with tears.

"I don't want to," she said, sorrow seeming to consume her body.

Oh, Hazel understood that to her core.

"But I know. I'll do it. I'll be you in a month," the girl promised, straightening her shoulders and trying to sit tall in her wheelchair.

"You will," Hazel said, even though she really shouldn't be promising anything back. She had no control over what the girl did. And yet Hazel felt a connection to her. She felt compelled to give her some small hope.

The girl managed a tiny smile before drooping again, her head resting on her own shoulder. Clearly she'd used up what little energy she had. Hazel hoped their interaction had been worth it.

She patted Chase's hand again and the boys continued wheeling her down the hall, stopping just in front of a bell. Hazel had longingly admired it after every treatment the past months, but today she was going to ring it.

Because she was done.

Hazel felt her family's presence close beside her as she reached a hand, trembling with both exhaustion and excitement, for the rope that dangled nearly to the floor.

She tugged once and the sweetest sound that had ever met her ears pealed through the hospital. Spontaneously she tugged again, but this time the sound of the bell was mixed with the raucous cheers of those around her.

She'd done it. She was at the end of the most terrible and yet most sacred time of her life. She'd learned so much about herself, been stretched beyond what she thought she was capable of, fought to live because she had to.

And even if she hadn't done these things by her own choice, she'd accomplished them. She was proud of the woman who'd be wheeling out of that hospital, even if she was too frail to walk and didn't have a hair on her body.

She glanced up at her grinning boys, each of their heads now thickly covered with hair even though they'd shaved them a few months prior. She heard her dad clear his throat, a sure sign he was holding back tears, and her mom sniffle, showing she'd lost the battle against her own tears.

She felt a kiss on the top of her head and looked up to see Wells smiling down on her. For over twenty years Hazel's sun had risen and set on that smile; her world had revolved around this man. It was strange how little of a reaction his smile now elicited in her. She appreciated him, but that was as far as her feelings went.

"I'm proud of you," he said.

She was proud of him too. He'd stepped up in a way she'd never dreamed possible, putting off recording a new album just so he could be with her and their boys during this time. She never would have asked that of him, but he'd done it despite her insistence that it wasn't necessary. Her gratitude for Wells went to Hazel's very core, even if she wasn't consumed with love for the man anymore.

Her heart lifted strangely at the realization. She wasn't in love with Wells anymore. At all. She had love for him as the father of her children and she really did wish him the best, but all of those incredible and destructive emotions she'd experienced as his wife and later as his ex-wife were gone. She was completely free.

When thinking about love, her mind couldn't help straying to Dylan. It wasn't until then that she'd realized her fear of cancer ending her life wasn't the only reason she'd pushed him away. Sure, she'd been fearful that Dylan would grow attached, only to lose her to this despicable disease. But it was much more than that. She was scared. Terrified that cancer would take away the one reason men had always chosen Hazel. It was no secret that people, especially men, thought Hazel to be beautiful. But when that disappeared, what did Hazel have left? Why would Dylan want to stay?

And yet the man now stood confidently with her family as if he belonged. And she guessed he did—he'd proven he would stay. She couldn't help wondering if he'd felt sorry for her, but even after telling herself that she couldn't help the way she felt. Because as much as she felt nothing for Wells, her heart grew with just the thought of Dylan. She felt everything for him.

It wasn't that she'd transferred her love for Wells to Dylan; that would be weird. But now that her heart wasn't in turmoil, full of fear and confusion over Wells—that was pretty much all she'd felt in the days after the divorce—she had room to let in all that Dylan created within her.

This was too much. Hazel leaned her head against the back of her wheelchair as the cheering died down.

"I think it's time to get her home," Wells said to the gathered group. As a country star, Wells was used to managing a crowd.

The hospital staff chuckled and began dispersing. Hazel was glad they'd all been there. She knew it couldn't be easy working with cancer patients, and watching these graduations was a reward for all of the time, effort, and tears they devoted to each of them.

Hazel felt her chair move again. The wheels turned left, toward the elevators and the promise of home.

"You did good, baby girl," Robert said from just above her head, telling Hazel that her sons had lost their job to her dad.

"You accomplished the near impossible," her mom added softly as she fell into step beside Hazel's chair. Tear tracks still marked her mother's cheeks.

"I am pretty danged awesome," Hazel agreed with her best attempt at a cocky grin, feeling the need to lighten the moment.

Her parents laughed, achieving her goal, and they all squeezed into one elevator.

The ride down was short and when they emerged Hazel noticed movement from the main lobby.

"For she's a jolly good fellow," Saffron began loudly as Callie hushed her.

They *had* come. Hazel shouldn't have doubted them.

"They didn't want us all up there," Laurel explained to Hazel as her dad wheeled her into the midst of her friends, who quickly surrounded her.

"I can't understand why," Kenzie said, nodding toward Saffron. "I mean, we're all so quiet and unassuming."

The group laughed, including Saffron, who didn't seem to mind the joke at her expense.

"Thank you," Hazel managed even though she was beyond weary at this point.

"You don't have to talk. You don't even have to listen to us. But we had to be here today," Callie said.

Hazel nodded. She was sure they knew she was showing her thanks with that slight movement.

"You are the best," Kenzie said as she dropped a kiss on the top of Hazel's head.

"You are one hell of a fighter," Saffron added as she patted Hazel's shoulder.

"And one hell of a winner," Callie added as she gave Hazel, along with the wheelchair, an awkward side hug.

"Love you," Laurel added, squeezing Hazel's hand lightly before they all stepped back and ushered Hazel on.

Hazel wanted them to all come with her—it felt weird leaving them behind when they'd come to see her—but she didn't have the energy to say any of that. She barely managed to raise her hand in goodbye.

Apparently all of the adrenaline that had come with ringing the bell had worn off, leaving her completely drained.

"Bye Grandma, bye Grandpa," Sterling and Chase called out as they began moving once more, and Hazel realized that her parents were leaving in another direction. She also heard Dylan and Wells say something but she was too tired to comprehend it.

Part of her wondered who was now wheeling her if her dad had left, but at this point she couldn't even open her eyes. She hoped whoever drove her home would know to keep the car warm. She was beginning to shiver once more.

More words were exchanged and Hazel realized she must have drifted off because she had no idea who had spoken or what they'd said. She was parked in her chair just outside the hospital entrance, but before she had time to wonder what was happening, Dylan's truck came into view.

His long body unfolded as he jumped out of the driver's seat and jogged toward where Hazel slumped in the wheelchair.

Despite her fatigue, she almost laughed as she watched him. She'd finally admitted to herself that she was head over heels in love with Dylan . . . but how could this gorgeous man be interested in a woman like her? He had beautiful, thick, salt and pepper (mostly pepper) locks, a stark contrast to her completely bald head. His skin was perpetually tanned, all the better to show off his body art that was tasteful yet gave just a hint of being a bad boy. Except that he wasn't. Not at all. Dylan Pinnegar was as good as men came. And she had the deepest feelings for him.

But could he really feel the same?

"Thanks, Ster," Dylan said as he slid to a stop in front of her chair, switching his energetic gait to slow, gentle movements as he reached for her.

After her catnap Hazel had a bit more strength, enough to turn her head and see that Sterling had stayed with her. Of course she hadn't been left alone. Yet it lifted her heart once again to see how her family was caring for her.

"I'll go catch up to Chase and Dad. Love you, Mom," Sterling called out. He waved and headed toward the parking garage.

"And you, sleeping beauty, are coming with me," Dylan said as he easily lifted Hazel into his arms.

"I can get into the car on my own," Hazel insisted, suddenly feeling shy. It had been one thing to think that Dylan could have been hers before, when she'd been vivacious and full of life, with curves and plenty of blonde hair. But now? Surely he was only sticking around because he felt sorry for her. That was the kind of heart Dylan had.

Of course, he'd insisted this wasn't the case, that even after the ravishment of chemo he thought she was beautiful. That he loved her. But Hazel didn't see how this was possible. Men as gorgeous as Dylan didn't date women who looked like she did now. They just didn't, unless they were in a romantic comedy, when reality was suspended.

But this was real life. And Dylan was in the majors while Hazel was on the bench in the little league.

"I don't really think you can. Besides, I didn't fight Wells for the opportunity to take you home just to miss this chance of having you in my arms," Dylan said with a wink.

He was saying all the words Hazel wanted to hear. Could he possibly mean them?

"That must have been quite the brawl." She managed a somewhat witty retort despite the growing headache that always followed her treatments.

"Oh, sweetheart, I'd never hit a man so physically beneath me," Dylan teased.

Hazel laughed. Wells had been living with her for the past five months and Dylan had insisted on sticking around as well, so this kind of verbal sparring had been part of her life for a while. But it still amused her, especially when Dylan came out on top. Wells the mega star could always use being brought down a notch . . . or three.

"The fight was more along the lines of Wells throwing a fit when I proposed that I take you and the boys go home with him. But when I got Sterling and Chase on my side, your ex didn't stand a chance."

Dylan loved to call Wells Hazel's ex. He said it proved the man was the most idiotic person on the planet. Anyone who let her go had to be.

Again, all the right words. He always said them—and swore he meant them—but even as Hazel hoped, she doubted. Not him, but herself. She couldn't believe that she could elicit such sentiments in a man, not when she was like this. But she still treasured every word.

So even as she hoped and dreamed that Dylan could really

feel for her what she felt for him, for now these sweet words were enough. She was too tired to even ask for more. But when she started feeling better, when she was well, would she ask then? Hazel couldn't answer that question.

But as Dylan cranked up the heater even though it was nearly eighty degrees outside, Hazel smiled in her heart. Maybe Dylan couldn't love her the way she loved him, but he cared. And as she drifted off to sleep she clung to that.

CHAPTER TWO

"I THINK that's it for today," Laurel said, standing up from her chair.

She always sat in the same chair in Riley's office. And although he'd sat across the desk from her in their first meetings, recently he'd taken the seat beside her. It had felt strange the first time and now that she was thinking about it, she wondered again. Why wasn't he in the fancy, ergonomic chair behind his desk? This was his office, after all.

Laurel dismissed the thought. She wasn't about to look a gift horse in the mouth, or more like analyze why her gift horse was behaving strangely. Riley had been a literal Godsend. Laurel's hope to compensate all of the people her ex Bennie had hurt with his false investments had been a pipe dream at first. But Riley was the one who'd sat down and had begun a plan, without her prompting. While Laurel was far from finished collecting funds from her own work, donations, and even a grant in one case, she had been able to restore lost investments to nearly a dozen of Bennie's victims. The number of people left to compensate was slowly dwindling and she now believed she would one day hit zero. All because of Riley.

"Yeah, good work," Riley said as he stood and stretched his broad shoulders.

Laurel couldn't help her quick perusal of Riley's fine form. Of course she'd always known Riley was attractive—he was the most sought after bachelor in town, after all—but this was different. Her heart flipped and her core warmed.

Surely it was only because she now admired Riley more than she ever had. Not only was he generously helping her, but he was also brilliant. The solutions and workarounds he'd proposed were nothing short of genius.

"Do you want to take any of this with you?" Riley pointed to the side table still laden with food.

The only way Laurel had agreed to accept Riley's help was if she could feed him. Her friends had said that on his busy days Riley often skipped lunch, so good, semi-healthy, and very comforting food was priceless to him. When Riley had volunteered to help her in her endeavor, she had countered with the offer to feed him. And feed him she did—typically with her chef friend Saffron's help, since Laurel usually used the kitchen at the inn that she and her friends owned. Well, they owned it and Laurel was working there until she could repay the portion Callie had fronted for Laurel. But who knew when that would be, since she was devoting every extra penny to those her ex had ripped off.

Laurel shook her head. "I don't think I'd be able to fit all that in my tiny fridge," she grinned.

Her new place might be small but it was all hers. For the first time in her life, Laurel was living alone. She had moved straight from her parents' home to Bennie's. And when everything had hit the fan with Bennie she'd moved in with Callie. Laurel and Callie loved each other, but Laurel knew that Callie was itching to get her house back to herself. Especially now that things were getting more serious with Leo, Callie's new boyfriend.

Thankfully an apartment on the outskirts of town had become available. It wasn't exactly the safest part of town, but then again Rosebud was pretty safe all around; even its more run-down parts weren't completely terrible.

So Laurel had a new place to call home, despite Callie's protests. Callie had begged her to stay until she could buy into the inn and then get her own place, but they both needed Laurel to move on. Callie needed to get her space back, and Laurel needed her independence.

She felt like Wonder Woman anytime she cooked, cleaned, or fixed something in the space that was all hers.

"I heard about your move," Riley said as he began to wrap up the food Laurel had brought.

It was some of her best work, if she said so herself. She'd created a Japanese fusion dish—kind of descriptive of Laurel herself—making Japanese-style hamburger steak but serving it with the best southern mashed potatoes on the west coast, along with Japanese-style spinach. It had been Saffron's brainchild but Laurel had cooked it herself . . . mostly. She had needed a little help with seasoning the gravy just right.

"Atlas Road is quite the neighborhood," Riley added, his dark eyes drifting upward to meet Laurel's.

Laurel nodded. "Yes, and I have quite the group of new neighbors. But I'm sure all of them were very grateful when I took them some of my homemade mochi." Laurel couldn't know for sure as no one had opened the door when she'd knocked, but the plates had all disappeared from the front steps, so she was going to take that as a sign of gratitude.

Riley shut his eyes for a moment and then opened them. "You took gifts to your neighbors on Atlas Road?" he asked, his voice slightly strained.

"It's what I've always done when I move into a new neighborhood. And the guy who lives on my right returned my plate to my doorstep along with a note to let me know that his rottweilers would now guard my place as well as his own." Laurel had been proud of that connection. The rest of the neighbors hadn't brought back the plates, but that was her fault for using real plates instead of disposable.

"Laurel," Riley said as he breathed out a sigh. "Do you know that most of my pro bono cases come from that area of town?"

"I imagine they need the help," Laurel said brightly.

Riley nodded. "They do. But it's not just a financial issue. It's also because the majority of our fair town's criminals live there. And it's where most of the domestic disturbances and drug deals happen." He spoke slowly, as if making sure Laurel understood what he was saying.

Laurel shrugged. "It wasn't the part of town I dreamed of living in, but it's the only place I can afford right now. And don't say I could have stayed with Callie. I really couldn't have intruded on her a day longer."

"I really doubt Callie thought of you as intruding. But okay, I get that. So let me help. If I funded some of this compensation you're insisting on, you could afford a part of town where you don't have to have three deadbolts on your door."

Laurel wasn't about to correct Riley and tell him that she had four. Surely they were only there because the landlord was extra conscious about security. Well, security he could afford. The closest thing Laurel had to cameras or an alarm were her neighbor's rottweilers.

"Not happening, Riley. You're already doing too much as it is," Laurel said adamantly. She hefted her purse onto her shoulder determinedly to emphasize that the discussion was over as far as she was concerned.

Riley shook his head and she could have sworn he muttered, "I would do so much more if you'd only let me."

But his voice was so quiet Laurel couldn't be sure, so she put it out of her mind, focusing on what he was saying now.

"Who really should be helping you out is Bennie." Riley's eyebrows drew together.

Laurel couldn't agree more. But considering that Bennie was in prison without a dime to his name and no way of making any money in the next five to seven years, she wasn't holding her breath for his help. He was so broke that the judge couldn't even order him to pay Laurel alimony. What a far fall from the wealthy lifestyle they'd led, a lifestyle that still ate away at Laurel, considering it had been funded by the money of the poor people she was now trying to help.

"He has nothing to give me," Laurel replied with a little shrug.

She had been angry at Bennie for a long time. Just a few months earlier those words would have been emotionally charged. But after time and reflection, Laurel had realized that feeding her anger helped no one. Her emotions would be better used by focusing on the needs of Bennie's victims. So that was what she was doing.

"So the divorce is final?" Riley asked.

"It went pretty quickly when Bennie didn't contest it, and since we have no assets to fight over," Laurel tried to joke, but it kind of fell flat. Probably because the situation was so sad.

"At least he was man enough to let you go," Riley said.

Laurel had to agree. For all of Bennie's faults, she appreciated that he'd known when it was time to let go, even if he'd refused to file for divorce himself. If she wanted it, he'd told her, she would have to do it. That had been one of the hardest decisions of Laurel's life, even after all Bennie had done. She'd grown up believing that marriage was a lifetime commitment and had struggled with guilt, pain, and shame over ending it. But even her parents had supported her when she'd made her final decision.

"Yeah, he was."

"And I, for one, am grateful he wasn't man enough to keep you," Riley added.

Laurel froze, replaying his words in her mind. It sounded like he was glad that Bennie was no longer with Laurel—that she was now free. Why would he care unless . . . no. It couldn't be. It had to be that he saw that Laurel was happier without her ex, and as her friend he wanted that for her. Right?

Right?!

Panic rose in Laurel's chest even as she scoffed at it. No way could the most eligible bachelor in town be interested in her. She was an aging mother of three grown children, with a criminal ex to boot. That kind of baggage deserved its own zip code. Riley could have any woman in town, including those who were too young to have accumulated the mess Laurel carried around with her daily. Well, mess and blessings. Those three grown children were Laurel's world.

"Breathe, Laurel," Riley said as she still stood frozen, though her mind was whirling. He took a step closer but refrained from touching her. She was grateful for that—or mostly grateful. She worried at the kind of reaction she'd have at his touch . . . while another part of her, a part she tried to ignore, wanted to find out.

Riley was charming, kind, handsome, smart, employed, and seemed to truly care about her. In just that partial list of his amazing traits, he had Bennie beat by like five. But that meant he was too good for her. If Laurel had attracted a man like Bennie, that must be the kind of man on her level. It was just logical.

"Please breathe," Riley urged again. This time concern etched his features.

Right. Laurel opened her mouth and let in a fresh breath.

"Thank you," Riley said, the tension on his face slacking though he still watched her carefully.

Air did feel good. Thank heavens for Riley.

"So I'm going to take it that if I ask you out right now, I'll get a repeat performance of the whole not-breathing thing," he said, completely shocking Laurel.

If she thought she was frozen before, that was nothing compared to how she felt now. Even her blood seemed to stop flowing.

"I'm not asking you out," Riley reiterated as he stretched his hands out just short of touching Laurel. "I need you to breathe for me again."

She opened her mouth. Oxygen filled her lungs.

Why was this so hard today?

"But I need you to know that I want to do it. I really like you, Laurel." Riley looked at her with his heart in his eyes, then sighed. "Maybe use your nose? I find it works better than my mouth."

How could he jump from revealing his feelings to teaching her how to breathe? He saw what a mess she was. Like right in this instance . . . major mess.

"I don't—you don't—" Laurel began, unable to get out a coherent sentence. It wasn't surprising, considering she could barely put together a coherent thought.

"I do. And I'm going to ask you out when you're ready. But I figured I'd give you a head's up. Then maybe you'll be ready sooner," Riley said with a wink that finally got Laurel's blood moving. Maybe moving too fast, actually. Could blood really boil? But she wasn't angry. She was . . . what was she?

"Is this a joke?" Laurel finally managed.

Riley grinned, shaking his head. "I've never been more serious about anything in my life."

Laurel shook her head too, but hers was in doubt. "Are you sure you're talking to the right woman?"

Riley barked out a laugh. "More than you'll ever know."

Laurel shook her head again wordlessly. This couldn't be happening. She'd just gotten divorced. Or at least recently enough that she shouldn't be considering dating again, right?

Because that was a big part of the problem. She was actually considering it. If Riley had risked her going into heart failure and had asked her out that day . . . Laurel might have said yes.

Oh dear heavens.

CHAPTER THREE

"HEY SAFF," Laurel called out from her typical spot at the check-in desk.

Although the Lodge now had more than enough staff to man the desk without the help of Laurel, Callie, or Kenzie, Saffron still saw each of the three behind the desk from time to time, Laurel most of all. Saffron was sure it was because Laurel liked to keep her finger on the pulse of operations. After their incident earlier that year when someone had attempted to sabotage the Lodge's reservations—and nearly succeeded in destroying their new business—she still seemed on high alert. Saffron knew Laurel had felt the whole thing was her fault, but it hadn't been. It had been retaliation against her ex Bennie, and Saffron hoped Laurel would able to relax soon.

"How's it going?" Saffron asked, leaning her arms on the standing-height desk that was currently devoid of guests.

Saffron came into work at noon on the days she worked closing at the restaurant. Now that they served three meals a day, closing meant she'd be there until at least ten that night. But since morning check-out time was at ten and check-in was at three, noon was typically a pretty slow time at the front desk.

"Really well," Laurel said, looking up from the computer. "We already have a full house for this entire month, and reservations for the rest of summer are filling up fast." She grinned.

Saffron returned it. Things were looking good on her end as well. Even though the restaurant now served three meals a day, there was often a waitlist to get in. It was a dream come true; things were finally humming along the way she'd always hoped. Well, at least in her professional life. Her personal life was another story.

"How was your meeting with Riley?" Saffron asked. She hadn't seen Laurel since she'd helped her whip up that beautiful lunch the day before.

"It was great. I think Callie wants to see you before you go to the kitchen." Laurel suddenly seemed engrossed with whatever was on her computer screen.

Saffron looked at her suspiciously. Clearly Laurel was hiding something, but since it was already a few minutes after noon and she still needed to check in with Callie, investigation would have to wait.

"Is she back there?" Saffron pointed to the offices where Callie and Kenzie typically worked unless they were putting out some sort of fire. Which was actually more often than not.

Laurel nodded, her eyes still riveted on the computer.

"I guess I'd better go see her. But don't think you're off the hook," Saffron warned. Laurel pretended to ignore her but Saffron knew she'd heard. With a sigh Saffron maneuvered around the desk and went in search of Callie.

The management space behind the front desk wasn't a huge area. It was just large enough to hold an office for whichever of the girls needed it—usually Callie and Kenzie—along with another office for the management they'd newly hired and a small breakroom. A door immediately behind reception led into a small corridor that housed the three offices. When Saffron walked in, all three doors were open, so she ventured without knocking into the office where she knew Callie would be.

"You needed to see me, Boss?" Saffron asked, feeling a little sassy. She knew Callie hated the term.

"Call me that again and you'll find yourself unemployed," Callie muttered as she shuffled through paperwork.

"You can't fire me," Saffron said in a sing-song voice. "I co-own the joint."

"Exactly. Which is why you can't call me boss," Callie countered, looking up with a winning smile on her face.

Saffron had walked right into that one. Point for Callie.

"Touché," she replied, conceding defeat. "But I really should be heading to the kitchen. Laurel said you wanted something?"

Callie shrugged. "I didn't need to see you."

Saffron grunted. Laurel. The sweet friend. It was always the sweet ones you had to watch out for.

"What happened?" Callie asked, her voice only half interested. Saffron was guessing that the paperwork in front of her had to do with a real estate deal. Working at the inn while maintaining her thriving real estate company couldn't be easy, but Callie somehow managed it with grace. Like she did with everything.

"I asked Laurel about her meeting with Riley. She just said that it was 'great' and then told me you needed to see me," Saffron explained.

Callie dropped her paperwork, finally looking up. "That's interesting."

"Exactly what I thought. Well, the kitchen can wait. I'm about to do some digging." Saffron smirked as she retreated from Callie's office.

"Pass the info on when you get it," Callie said before burying herself in the documents again.

"Will do," Saffron replied as she opened the door to return to the lobby.

But the stinker was gone. In her place was Jenny, their staff manager.

Well played, Laurel, Saffron thought as she made her way to the kitchen. But Laurel would have to surface at some point and when she did, Saffron would pounce.

The kitchen was humming with activity when Saffron entered. A peek into the dining room had shown that nearly all of the tables were taken, so her staff were understandably busy. She took in the work her line cooks were doing and the way Saffron's newest hire, Nick, was managing them. So far so good. She was impressed by them all.

Things were moving seamlessly for her. Well, seamlessly as long as she kept her personal life separate from her professional life.

Speaking of which . . . Saffron quickly scanned the kitchen and frowned. Where was Alex? He should have been here this morning since he was working the opposite shift she was. He'd been doing that for the past couple of months, at his girlfriend's request.

Saffron sighed. She knew she hadn't had to give in to Cherry. The woman had no right dictating what happened in Saffron's kitchen. But Saffron had done it to keep the peace and because she felt a fair amount of guilt for lusting after Cherry's boyfriend. Besides, she'd already given up so much for the woman, so why not this too?

When Alex had begun dating Cherry, Saffron had told herself it was a good thing. There had been a moment there, just before Alex suddenly gained a new girlfriend, when Saffron had been over at his house, visiting his mom. She hadn't gone to see him, but then Paula had gone to bed and Saffron and Alex had been left alone. He would have kissed her, she was sure of it, had she not pulled back at the last second. She'd completely lost her head, pining for her coworker for too long. But even she knew better than to kiss Alex while he worked for her. It could be a legal mess, not to mention that it was just plain wrong.

Alex had spent the better part of a week avoiding any interaction with Saffron and she hadn't known how to repair things. But then Cherry had come along. And it felt for a time like things were getting back to normal, until Cherry had claimed she felt uncomfortable with how much time Saffron spent with Alex's mom. Cherry had said it undermined the relationship she was trying to build with Paula. And Saffron guessed she could understand that, even if it didn't seem fair to her or to Paula. So she stopped visiting, and both of them missed it terribly.

Paula still texted Saffron daily, mostly with updates about how Cherry was making her life miserable. But even Paula had agreed that it was best to go along with Cherry's wishes. That didn't really surprise Saffron; Paula had always been big on keeping the peace. Even though she had been the first one to try to match Saffron and Alex up, Paula knew that this dream would never come true.

So they'd found a new normal. Saffron's friendship with Paula was surviving on texts, and as for her relationship with Alex, even though they worked together, Saffron barely saw him since they now worked opposite shifts.

But things had changed about a month before when Saffron had hired Nick. Previously, it had been easy for Alex and Saffron to avoid each other at work because one had to open and the other had to close. But with three of them, their schedules overlapped much more. And things with Alex felt like they were getting better. They were back to joking and being the kind of coworkers Saffron had always wanted them to be.

Then one day Alex had sheepishly come to Saffron and

voiced more of Cherry's wishes. She didn't want him working so closely with Saffron. The underlying meaning had been clear and Saffron wasn't sure she'd ever been more embarrassed. Cherry had seen right through Saffron's façade, figuring out that she liked Alex, and wanted to squash it. If Cherry could see it, did everyone else? Were all of her employees talking about how pathetic she was behind her back? Saffron couldn't completely blame them. She was pathetic, especially after she gave in to Cherry so that now Alex always opened and she always closed.

But despite Cherry's demands, Alex didn't usually leave until he'd given Saffron a report on how things had gone and what she should know going into her shift, as well as just saying hi. Besides, he was supposed to be working until three today. He still had three hours left on the clock. Was he taking his lunch break?

"There was a situation," Nick explained as he joined Saffron where she stood overlooking her kitchen.

Saffron's heartrate increased, all thoughts of Alex fleeing. What had happened? Why hadn't she been called in?

"Is everyone okay?" she asked anxiously.

"Physically, yeah. We were all just a little startled," Nick said, pausing to crack his neck as if he hated being the bearer of this news.

Now all Saffron felt was curiosity. What had happened?

"She came in spitting mad." Raquel joined the conversation and Saffron realized she needed to discuss this somewhere else if she didn't want her whole staff pausing their work.

"How about we talk about this in my office?" Saffron asked Nick as Raquel frowned.

Saffron loved Kenzie's sister almost like her own, but the woman could be distracted by the wind. If Saffron let Raquel join the conversation, who knew when she'd get back to work. Saffron had learned the hard way that the trick to keep Raquel on task was to never give her a chance to get off task. Simple, but also difficult. Because this was Raquel.

Saffron noticed many of the hands in the kitchen had stilled.

"Everyone else back to work," Saffron barked and the sounds of a hardworking kitchen filled her ears once more.

She was known for running a tight kitchen, and she knew the staff liked it when Alex was in charge more than when she was. She didn't blame them. Alex was the fun uncle, while Saffron was the tough single mom. But someone had to keep them all in check. She cared deeply for each of her staff, but she wasn't about to let them goof off. To be fair, Alex didn't either, but he also gave some leeway that Saffron didn't.

So far it was working for them. Alex could be easier on the staff in the morning and then Saffron would make sure everything got done in the evening. Despite a little grumbling, she was pretty sure her employees respected her for it.

"So what happened?" Saffron asked when they were in her office, safely away from listening ears.

"Cherry," was all Nick had to say. Saffron could only imagine the kind of chaos Cherry had brought to her kitchen.

"She came here? While he was working?" Saffron's eyes were wide. The woman had always been audacious but this went beyond even what Saffron had thought she would do.

Nick nodded.

"She was ranting and raving. Her words were kind of slurred and I couldn't tell if she was really upset or completely smashed," Nick said.

Saffron's eyes closed in complete mortification for Alex. She wasn't sure where the two of them stood, but she did know she wanted the best for him. More than ever, she was sure that Cherry wasn't it. But it wasn't her decision.

"Just a head's up, I heard your name a time or two," Nick

said. He pursed his lips and his gaze dropped to the floor as if he didn't relish delivering that information.

"Meaning all of the staff heard as well," Saffron groaned.

Nick nodded.

"The good news is I couldn't tell what she said about you. But the bad news is it was implied that you were the reason she was so upset." Nick leaned against the wall, looking at Saffron sympathetically.

"Ugh, why? I have literally done everything she's asked." Saffron fell back into her seat, grateful she'd opted for a soft-back chair. Something harder would have definitely left a mark.

Nick shrugged.

"Anything else?" Saffron sighed. She didn't want to ask but Nick's body language said he wasn't quite done.

"You know I hate to gossip, especially about my coworkers. I'm only telling you this because it was said for all of us to hear and I don't want you to be blindsided," Nick said, shifting so that his shoulder was now against the wall.

Although Saffron didn't know Nick well, she knew he was telling the truth. In the month he'd worked for her he'd been completely professional.

Saffron nodded and braced herself. The other part had been hard enough to hear and Nick hadn't hesitated to share it. So what was coming had to be worse.

"Alex is quitting."

Saffron felt her stomach drop as she struggled to keep her expression neutral. She fought a stab of physical pain at the news.

"Oh," Saffron managed as Nick cracked his neck again uncomfortably.

Saffron drew in a deep breath, realizing she could show some emotion. Any head chef would be devastated by the news that their sous would be leaving. Especially one that was relied on so heavily. Surely no one would fault her for showing how upset she was . . . even though the complete and utter loss she felt at the words 'Alex is quitting' had very little to do with the kitchen. The kitchen would survive. Nick was amazing and they had a list of applicants twenty deep who'd be chomping at the bit for Alex's job. The issue wasn't the kitchen. It was Saffron's heart.

She knew she couldn't be with Alex while he worked for her. But she'd still been able to keep him in her life. But now? Now he'd leave with Cherry on his arm and without a backward glance. Whatever was between Saffron and Alex, no matter how weird, was all she'd had. And now that was gone. She took a deep breath to compose herself and looked at Nick.

"Are you sure?" Saffron asked calmly. Even if she didn't need to act unaffected for her reputation's sake, she needed to keep the emotion at bay so she didn't completely fall apart.

"Those were some of the only sentences I understood from Cherry. Something about if Alex already has another job lined up, why hasn't he quit yet?"

He already had another job. So Alex had been planning this and hadn't felt the need to give Saffron any advanced notice. Was he gone for good? Was this public argument his way of quitting?

No, she couldn't believe that. Those actions weren't like the man she knew. Although since Cherry had entered his life, she'd only caught glimpses of the man she knew.

"Thank you," Saffron managed with a brief nod. She hoped Nick would get the hint and go back to the kitchen. Her hold on her emotions was beginning to slip.

Nick offered her a sympathetic smile. "I can work extra hours while we figure things out."

Saffron knew what a sacrifice he was making for her. "Thank you. I will probably have to take you up on that."

Nick nodded, a slight frown creasing his forehead. Saffron wasn't the only one Alex was leaving in the lurch.

Nick turned to leave, but before he could open the door a knock sounded.

"Saff?" Alex's voice called out.

No. Not now. She was literally about to lose it. And the last thing she wanted was for Alex to witness that. She needed help, a support system. Poor Nick would have to do.

"Do you mind staying?" Saffron's voice squeaked as she turned to Nick desperately.

"Not at all." Nick pointed his thumb toward the door. "You want me to get that?"

Saffron nodded and drew herself up, gathering every ounce of inner strength. She could hold on for about a minute. And then Alex needed to be gone.

She'd thought they were at least friends . . . she felt moisture begin to well in her eyes.

Nope, no thoughts like that. Not until later.

"Oh, hey, Nick. Mind if I talk to Saffron for a sec?" Alex asked, the picture of ease as he strode into Saffron's office.

"I've asked Nick to stay," Saffron said, her voice cold. She couldn't help it. The only way to avoid breaking down was to suppress her emotions, which just left a cold outer shell. But Alex could deal with it. All he had to do was say he was quitting and then he could leave. And then she could deal with it alone.

"I'd prefer to have this conversation in private," Alex said, trying to meet Saffron's gaze. She kept her eyes averted.

"I already know you're quitting," Saffron said, her voice cracking. She cleared her throat and then looked at Alex expectantly. Why was this conversation taking so long?

"I had hoped to tell you myself." Alex frowned at Nick but Saffron wouldn't allow that.

"It wasn't his fault he overheard your girlfriend going on a tirade in the middle of *my* kitchen."

At least Alex looked ashamed at those words.

"Look, can we please talk? Alone?" Alex was almost begging. He stepped forward until he was against Saffron's desk, his legs against the tabletop as he leaned toward her imploringly.

That would have worked . . . ten minutes before. But it was too late now.

"If you're done here, I don't think there is anything more to say," Saffron countered. She shifted against the back of her chair, needing to distance herself from Alex as much as possible.

Fire glinted in Alex's eyes. Where did he get the right to be angry?

"You don't?" he asked.

His fire ignited one within Saffron as well. She was the one who should be upset.

Saffron shook her head. "In fact, I think it would be best if you left my kitchen immediately." She crossed her arms over her chest.

"I'm quitting, Saffron. That means nothing to you?" Alex searched her face, as if hoping she would hear an underlying meaning to his words. But what could it be? That Cherry had finally taken control of every part of his life?

Saffron felt her short-lived anger giving way to intense sadness. She was running out of time.

"I think you should go," Nick interjected, taking a step toward Alex.

"Maybe you should go," Alex countered.

"Both of you, go." Saffron managed to still sound cold and in control.

Thank goodness.

"Saff." Alex had some nerve, using her nickname with that tone.

She dropped her eyes. She couldn't bear to watch him leave. Surely he'd known what she felt for him. And she understood why he'd latched onto Cherry, since Saffron couldn't be with him while they worked together. But he was leaving. So why was he continuing to choose Cherry instead of her? Well, they could have a happily ever after in hell for all Saffron cared. Maybe if she kept repeating that she'd actually believe she didn't care.

Saffron heard the door open but kept her eyes firmly glued to her desk.

"You really should respect her wishes, man. And since you are no longer an employee, you can't be in the kitchen," Nick added. He was the guardian angel Saffron needed at the moment.

"I still have two weeks," Alex began, but Saffron wasn't having it. She raised her gaze as high as she dared, still unable to meet his eyes. But her voice was clear.

"No you don't. Either you quit today or I fire you." Saffron felt a little of that anger again but she knew it wouldn't last for long. Alex needed to leave now.

He lingered in the doorway and Saffron kept her eyes on his firm chest. She wouldn't be able to follow through on her threat if she looked into his eyes. But she had to keep her word. If he wouldn't leave, she'd have to make him. If not, she'd look like a lovesick fool in front of all of her employees, and that couldn't happen.

"I'm not done. We'll talk about this later," Alex promised before he finally walked away.

Saffron leaned over her desk wearily as she heard Nick's heavy tread leaving her office as well. The door closed, finally leaving her in blessed peace. If only she actually felt peaceful.

. . .

CALLIE HADN'T BEEN to a drive-in movie since she was a teen. She'd gone with her girls but had secretly hoped to run into her crush, Donovan Johnson, after overhearing him say that he was going to the same movie that night.

Donovan had ended up being a no-show and the next week he'd started dating Candy Johnson. Callie had always thought it was stupid that they'd dated when they had the same last name. Didn't that mean they were related? It may have been generations before, but they came from the same family.

She'd enjoyed the movie regardless, but she was sure tonight would be even better. Because she'd be with Leo. She loved that he didn't do the typical fancy, monotonous dinner for all of their dates. In Callie's experience, once men hit age forty they lost any semblance of creativity. Thus all of her dates for the last ten years had been the same boring dinner. But Leo was different. Maybe because he was only a few years past forty? Callie grinned. She kind of loved dating a younger man.

"So I didn't check the movie listings until today, and I'm not sure you're going to like our options," Leo said as he drove toward the west side of town. The drive-in had been there for at least fifty years and despite extraordinary offers, they'd refused to sell. As a real estate agent Callie hoped to one day be a part of that transaction—it would be huge and it was inevitable. Even if the current owners were intent on keeping things the way they were, Callie doubted the next generation would care so deeply. She saw it all the time. But as a movie-goer and Rosebud resident, she was relieved that the owners had maintained such a historic part of their town and hoped things wouldn't change anytime soon.

"I actually have no idea what's in theaters right now," Callie admitted. Between her two jobs, friends, family, and dating Leo, she didn't exactly have time to watch trailers, let alone go to a theater. And on the rare occasions Callie did have time to relax she was more of a book woman.

"That's a good thing. Because the drive-in is doing Christmas in May," Leo said with a chuckle.

Callie joined him in laughter. That was a first. Marketing knew no bounds these days.

"What does that even mean?" she asked, shaking her head.

"My thoughts exactly. But apparently it means showing Christmas movies in May. We have the options of *It's a Wonderful Life*, *White Christmas*, *Home Alone*, or *Die Hard*," Leo replied.

"Classics," Callie grinned. It was strange, but she was on board.

Leo smiled back. "You still want to try it? It's not too late to change plans."

"I just wish I'd worn something festive," she joked. "Which one are we seeing?"

"The choice is yours, my love," Leo replied, causing Callie's heart to flip.

They'd exchanged the words *I love you* a month, two weeks, and four days before and ever since that momentous occasion Leo had often called Callie his love. It thrilled her every danged time.

"I don't really feel like crying," Callie said after she got control over her flipping heart.

"So that's a no to *It's a Wonderful Life* or *Die Hard*," Leo deadpanned.

Callie burst into laughter.

"How about *White Christmas*?" she finally suggested.

"Sounds good to me," Leo said as he pulled into line. They were only the second in line, which didn't surprise Callie. She wasn't sure this Christmas in May promo was the smartest idea.

Leo bought their ticket and drove to the screen, finding a spot rather easily since there were only four other cars in the entire lot.

"This can't be good for business," Callie frowned, looking around at all of the empty spots.

"From what I heard, the Donaldsons aren't hurting for cash now that they've sold half of their land," Leo replied.

Callie hadn't known that. How had she missed such a huge transaction? It had probably happened while they were dealing with their issues at the Lodge. But she realized she needed to keep a better pulse on the real estate market in town. Because it was already starting. The Rosebud resident in her was glad only half of the land had been sold off. The agent in her was annoyed she'd missed that sale.

"You sure do know a lot about Rosebud, considering I live here and you don't," Callie said as she leaned toward the middle of the car.

Leo took her hand and kissed the back of it.

Callie couldn't help her happy sigh.

"My job kind of keeps me in the loop," Leo said as he continued to hold Callie's hand, his thumb drawing small circles on her palm.

This had to be what heaven was like.

"I guess that makes sense," Callie agreed. She knew how much Leo worked in Rosebud, since she'd met him while he was working on the Lodge. It made sense that his construction business would take him all over the area.

"Do you mind passing me a sandwich?" Leo asked, pointing their joined hands toward a brown paper bag at Callie's feet.

Callie was loath to let go of Leo's hand but she also didn't want her man to starve. Reluctantly she pulled away and dug through the bag full of takeout. Leo had picked up three subs, two salads, and multiple desserts from one of her favorite delis.

"You did know that you were ordering for only two, right?" Callie teased.

"Don't underestimate my ability to eat," Leo joked right back as she handed him the biggest sandwich. She had no idea what kind it was but thought he would appreciate the size.

He glanced at the wrapper before opening it.

"I thought you loved club sandwiches," he commented in a questioning tone as Callie brought out another sandwich. She turned it over and saw that it was labeled roast beef.

"I do," Callie agreed. "But that thing is as big as my head."

Leo nodded. "Exactly. That means it's good."

Callie giggled. She wasn't sure she'd ever get used to Leo rating quantity as the most important characteristic when choosing food. The guys she'd dated in the past had always ranked food according to quality. But Leo said that in his line of work the most crucial thing was how well something filled the stomach.

"Then I'll let you have that good one. And I'll have the not-so-good roast beef." Callie held up her sandwich next to his to show its lacking size.

"If you insist," Leo said with a grin before he tore off the wrapper and dug in.

Callie watched Leo eat with gusto and realized that was how he took on all of life. And she adored that about him. He tore into things; he didn't do anything halfway.

For that reason she was a little surprised that they'd been dating for nearly five months and had yet to discuss their future in any way, shape, or form. Sure, they planned dates, but never further out than a week. The most serious conversation they'd had was when they'd said the L-word for the first time—and even that conversation hadn't promised anything more. It was fine . . . for now. But Callie wondered what Leo thought about their future. Or if he thought about it. He had to have considered it, right?

Callie knew she did. Daily. Maybe you couldn't put a timeline on love, but she'd always dreamed of a spring wedding. Next spring would be perfect: that gave them a year to grow closer, for Leo to propose, and then for her to plan a wedding.

Maybe Callie was wanting too much, too fast, but at her age she didn't want to wait around for years to see if things would work. She loved Leo, and he loved her. For her that was enough to move to the next step. Dating was fun, but she'd dated for thirty-five years now. She wanted more. Soon.

Did Leo?

It wasn't like she needed a proposal today. She understood if Leo wasn't quite there yet. Most men wouldn't be. But she wanted to talk about their future. To share where they saw themselves, to confirm that they were at least on the same path toward the goal Callie wished for. A summer wedding could be nice too, if Leo needed a slightly longer timeline.

"Looks like some deep thoughts you've got going there." Leo turned to Callie midbite, his head cocked as he scrutinized her face. If that wasn't love, she didn't know what was. The man didn't let much get between himself and his food.

She considered her response. Would it be pushy to bring up what she'd been thinking? He had asked, after all. And Leo loved her. He wouldn't freak out. She knew lots of women waited for a man to make the first move, but that wasn't Callie. It never had been.

"Where do you see this going?" Callie asked.

Leo's wide eyes were the only sign he was startled before he rubbed a hand over the five-o'clock shadow that Callie loved.

"I'm guessing you don't mean the movie," he replied.

"We never talk about the future. And I've been fine with

living in the moment. I still will be. But it would be nice to know what you think about us."

"What I think about us," Leo mused as the movie began to play. But instead of turning up the radio so they could hear the audio from the movie, Leo turned it down.

Callie grinned. She should have known Leo would take this seriously.

"I think I like spending time with you," Leo began with a small smile.

"I think I like spending time with you too," Callie replied, her smile a little wider.

His grew in response.

"I think you're the best thing that has happened to me in a long time," Leo continued.

Callie felt her smile dip. It made sense that he said that. He had children. Of course they were the best thing to *ever* happen to him. That was how it should be, how Callie wanted it to be . . . or told herself she wanted it. But to hear it aloud was a little tough.

"No reciprocating?" Leo teased, not seeming to understand her quietness.

She decided not to get into that now. She didn't want Leo to misunderstand her hurt and think she wanted him to put her before his kids. It was just hard to come second place to anyone, even to those who deserved first place. But she was sure that with time this part of their relationship would work out just fine. Callie just needed to get used to dating a dad. She'd rarely done so before, but Leo's devotion to his children was one of the things Callie loved most about him. Speaking of which . . .

"When am I going to meet your kids?" Callie asked.

That was another subject they'd avoided. Both kids were now teens so date nights had been easy. There was no worry about babysitters and bedtimes, and he only spoke about them as a part of his life, not as a part of his life he wanted to include her in. She'd forgotten how that bugged her until this very moment.

If he loved them and he loved her, shouldn't he want them all to get to know one another?

"Um," Leo said in a way that Callie didn't like. A way that said he was going to put her off.

"It just doesn't feel like the right time," he said, as gently as possible.

Okay, Callie could understand that.

"But we're planning on it, right? Like, do you have a time-line in your head?" Callie asked and then watched as Leo's eyes shuttered. "A very loose timeline?" she amended.

"They're kids, Callie. They just went through their parents' divorce." Leo glanced away uncomfortably.

'Just' was a relative term. Leo's divorce had been finalized recently but it had dragged on for years. The kids had known their parents were getting divorced at least two years before. Wasn't that long enough to get used to the idea? But even as Callie wondered, she refrained from voicing her thoughts. Leo was right; they were kids. Callie needed to be sensitive to their needs more than her own.

"I guess I'm getting a little ahead of myself," she admitted, trying not to sound disappointed.

Leo's smile was one of pure relief.

"I mean, I have to meet them at some point. I can be patient," Callie added.

"Hm," Leo grunted.

What the heck did that mean?

"You are planning on one day introducing me to them." Callie said it as a fact because there was no other way forward.

"Callie, you are one part of my life," Leo began.

Callie felt her whole body close in as she cringed.

"An important part of my life," he amended, but the damage had been done.

"It's just, I don't see why the two sides of my life have to mix." Leo seemed finished but Callie felt they'd barely begun.

"Like work and home life," Callie reasoned, but even as she said the words they didn't make sense. Work and home were so different from a girlfriend and his children.

"Exactly," Leo confirmed with a quick nod.

"So am I work? Obviously your kids are home," Callie continued. If Leo wanted to go with this analogy she was going to let him finish it. He'd realize it didn't hold up.

"I guess. I love my work," Leo said, as if that would make everything better.

Callie felt her emotions rising in her throat but tried to keep them down. She understood what Leo was saying—heck, she'd introduced the analogy. But he had to see how wrong it was, didn't he?

"But I'm going to have to merge with your kids at some point. When we get more serious." Callie realized she was heading toward the conversation she'd initially been avoiding. Leo wanted marriage one day too, didn't he? She'd always assumed it, but hearing he wasn't planning to ever introduce his kids to Callie changed things and she wasn't sure about anything now.

"We are serious," Leo said. "Way more serious than I would have ever imagined myself being with anyone after my divorce."

Callie nodded. They were way more serious than she'd imagined as well. But at the same time, not serious enough for long term. Dating wasn't her end goal. It seemed like Leo was being purposefully dense, so she was going to have to spell it out for him.

"More serious, Leo. As in engagement, and one day . . . marriage." Callie swallowed and pushed her hair behind her ear nervously. These weren't the ideal circumstances to be talking about this but it had to be said.

"Oh," Leo responded. His entire body shifted so that he was leaning against the door of his truck, as far from Callie as possible in the tight quarters.

Suddenly it all became clear: the avoidance of talking about their future, not seeing a need to introduce her to his kids, her being his 'work' . . .

"You aren't planning on any of that, are you?" Callie asked, her voice dwindling to a whisper.

"It's just . . . I've been there, Callie. Done that. It doesn't work," Leo said with a shrug of his shoulders as if it was as easy as that. He'd explained and now she needed to comply.

"It *didn't* work," Callie amended as she leaned forward, trying to bridge the space Leo had put between them.

He didn't budge from his spot against the door. "I lived it. I saw how it destroyed my relationship with my ex. That pressure every day, it was just too much."

"For the two of you." Callie was desperate to make him see.

"For me," Leo concluded.

But Callie didn't like that conclusion.

"Marriage works for a lot of people," she argued.

"It doesn't work for just as many," Leo replied.

He wasn't wrong. But it was marriage. This was important to Callie, something she needed in the future of her relationship. It wasn't something she could explain in that moment, but the idea that it wasn't a possibility—ever—well, that couldn't happen. Callie couldn't handle that. She wanted to marry the man she loved. She couldn't stay in this place forever, the realm of date nights and late night phone calls, two separate lives touching base when possible. She needed good morning kisses and a commitment of forever.

"So you're saying if you hadn't married your ex, you'd still be together?" Callie asked.

Was he feeling regret? Did he want to get back together with his ex-wife?

"I see what you're thinking. And it's not about her at all. I don't know what would have happened with us if we had taken another road. I honestly don't care. What I do care about is you, and this relationship. And I can't stifle it with marriage."

"Marriage doesn't stifle a relationship. It helps it to bloom!" Callie knew she was getting overly passionate but she couldn't stand this. Leo had to want marriage. The alternative wasn't a possibility.

"We're going to have to agree to disagree on this one. I am never going to see marriage the way you see it," Leo said. His voice was still gentle but he spoke firmly.

Callie's heart was in her stomach.

"And you won't ever get married again?" she whispered, tears already filling her eyes. She didn't want to ask the question but she had to know.

Leo shook his head slowly.

"Even if you love the woman? Can't live without her?" Callie begged.

"Especially then. I can't do that to someone I love. To you." The words reverberated in her head as Leo essentially promised that he would never marry her.

A lump formed in Callie's throat and she felt like she was going to be sick.

Could she give up marriage? Could she do it to stay with Leo? She'd made a promise to herself long ago that she'd never live with a man until they'd said their vows, but that wasn't exactly what Leo was proposing, was he? If this was as serious as they'd ever be, maybe he didn't even see it going that far. Probably not. Not if he planned on keeping his life in nice compartments. He lived with his kids. Callie wouldn't fit in that compartment.

The more she thought about it, the more she realized she couldn't do it. Wouldn't do it, even for a man she loved as much as Leo. It wasn't just the fantasy of a wedding. Marriage was so much more than that. It was exchanging lifelong vows, showing their friends, family, and God—and each other—that they were in this for better or worse.

She also realized that if they continued to date things would doubtless progress, at least physically if not in any other way. And Callie wanted that with a man. She'd dreamed about that kind of closeness with a man, with her husband. With Leo. But if she gave that part of herself to Leo without vowing to be together forever, she would be betraying the very fabric of what made Callie, Callie. She'd be giving up on a promise she made to herself, changing her identity for someone else . . . someone who wasn't willing to commit himself to her.

So here they were. At this impasse. Neither side able or willing—Callie wasn't sure which—to give more.

"I need the possibility of marriage, Leo. Not tomorrow, but you could one day change your mind, couldn't you?" Callie was begging now.

Leo was quiet, silence filling the car for too many minutes.

"I wish I could say that. But that would make me the kind of man unworthy of you, because it would be a lie. I'd only say it so that I wouldn't lose you. But I can't get married. I've seen it ruin too much."

"But there was a time you thought you wouldn't love again, wasn't there?" Callie didn't know that was the case but it made sense, considering his history.

"I didn't ever think that. As soon as I knew it was really over with my ex I hoped for a great love in my future. I hoped for you."

Callie had never truly understood the term 'heartbroken' until that moment, when she felt her heart shatter right there in her chest.

"Can't you give up the idea of what you wanted when you were a kid?" Leo asked.

But it was so much more than that. Marriage wasn't just some childhood dream. It was what she'd always aspired to. And a relationship that fell short of it? If she agreed to Leo's terms and kept seeing him, she worried she'd one day despise him for not giving her the one thing she wanted. If she gave in now she'd be doing the same thing that Leo said he wouldn't do to her: lying. She couldn't treat him like that.

"It's not that simple," Callie said, the tears now flowing down her cheeks.

"It never is. Choose us," Leo pleaded.

"I'm asking the same of you," Callie begged right back.

"We don't need to make a decision now," Leo said when he saw Callie wasn't budging.

"Except we do," Callie said. "Because now we know. We can't go back and pretend this conversation didn't happen. We have no future."

"That's not fair. We don't have the future you imagined. But I promise it would be beautiful."

"Beautiful? With me as work and your kids as home?" Callie scoffed.

Now she was getting angry. How dare he act as if all she had to do was give up some silly childhood desire, while he was only offering her part of himself instead of his whole heart?

"You would probably meet them someday," Leo replied.

Callie froze. Probably. Someday. Was that what they were going to build their relationship on?

She couldn't do this. She knew no man was perfect, but this wasn't something they could overcome. They'd grow to resent each other and inevitably would one day find they had something far worse than the end of Leo's marriage had been. Something that should have never begun.

"Take me home," Callie managed through her tears.

"Don't do this," Leo urged, finally moving away from the truck door, leaning toward her.

But she had to. For herself, and also for him.

"We want different things."

"I want you," Leo said. He reached a hand toward her and she felt her anger melting away. She wanted him too. The worst part was that Leo had been nearly perfect. Why did his one downfall have to be insurmountable?

Was she being overly dramatic?

But she knew the truth. This was something neither could change. It went deep. For Callie, she felt it to her core. Marriage was a need, not a want, for her future if she was in a relationship where she was happy.

And Leo couldn't give that to her. Clearly this wasn't just a flippant choice for him either.

"So you're saying you want marriage more than you want me?" Leo snapped as he jerked his truck into reverse.

Callie saw he'd found her old friend anger.

"The same way you're saying you can't do marriage even if it means losing me," Callie replied softly. She didn't want to fight, not if these were her last moments with Leo.

He lived in another town. Their paths might never cross again.

Or they would, some distant day in the future. They'd wave and remember what had almost been. Would Callie still be broken then? Would he have moved on?

Callie imagined the beauty on his arm who was willing to stay in her compartment, who didn't need marriage.

Lucky girl. But Callie knew she was doing the right thing

because even as she envied that woman, she knew she couldn't become her. Not if she wanted to be true to herself.

"We could maybe do some kind of a commitment ceremony," Leo proposed, but as soon as he said the words Callie knew he realized what she did. That would never work. They'd both be giving half to lose exactly what they were avoiding. Callie still wouldn't have her marriage and she'd resent that. Leo would have given into a ceremony he didn't believe in and he'd resent her.

"Can't love conquer all?" Leo asked as he wound through the dark roads toward Callie's home.

She shook her head. "Love can't conquer who we are. Then there would be no one left to love."

As Callie spoke the words, their truth hit her heart. Even as she hated them, she knew they were right. She knew she had to live by them, even if it meant giving up the only man she'd ever truly loved. Maybe the only man she ever would love.

CHAPTER FOUR

KENZIE STOOD IN HER KITCHEN, watching Bryan sit comfortably on her couch. There were two things wrong with that thought: *her* kitchen and *her* couch. She'd imagined that these things would have become *theirs* long before today.

They'd talked about Bryan moving back in nearly six months before. Raquel had moved out five months ago. And yet here they were, Bryan a guest in her home. Why? Kenzie couldn't help asking herself.

She gathered the cups of tea she'd been steeping and made her way to sit beside her guest. Ugh. It just wasn't right. Things were going so well with Bryan. She'd been trying to give him time, to resist her natural impulse of running headlong into things. But six months?

Every woman had her limit and Kenzie had passed hers long ago. She was just wondering if she was at the threshold for a normal woman yet. Because if she was there, she was going to press the issue. Granted, maybe some women had no limits. Maybe they would sit, patiently waiting forever. But Bryan knew who Kenzie was. She'd changed immensely, but this need to go after what she wanted was innate for Kenzie. If he couldn't handle that, he needed to find another woman.

Not that Kenzie wanted that. Through their months and months of working on their relationship, one thing stood out above all else: Bryan was the man for her. He always had been and he always would be. Did he push her buttons? Yes. Did they disagree? Yes. Did she annoy him? Heck yes. But despite that they both knew that this—them—was what they wanted. Yet now she was feeling unsure. If Bryan did want this to work, why wasn't he making the move into her home like they'd discussed?

Kenzie was driving herself bananas.

She glanced up to see Bryan staring at her.

Oops. She'd assumed he was still texting like he had been when she'd left to make tea.

"Out with it," Bryan said as Kenzie bit her lip.

No, she wouldn't say it. She was going to be demure. Thanks to therapy she was now Kenzie 2.0. The kind of woman who didn't demand things from her relationship. Kenzie didn't need to control—

"Why haven't you moved in yet?" she blurted and then sighed. So much for Kenzie 2.0.

Bryan grinned.

Kenzie fumed.

He thought this was funny? She was doing everything in her control to keep from doing this exact thing and yet he'd driven her to it.

Nope. Back up, Kenzie. He didn't drive her to do anything. If therapy had taught her anything it was that she made her own choices. Had Bryan's choice bugged her? Yes. Did she feel there was no other alternative because Bryan hadn't made the move? Yes. But did he make her do this? No. Even if she wanted to blame it all on him.

"I wanted to find the perfect time to do this tonight. But between my late arrival at the restaurant and then having the worst server on the planet . . . " Bryan began to explain, but Kenzie still didn't understand. What did the kid who served them the wrong food have to do with why Bryan wasn't moving in?

"And then I wanted to go to the beach after dinner but you had to pee," Bryan continued.

"The beach is like an hour away and the bathrooms there are so gross." Kenzie defended herself even if she wasn't sure why.

"I get it. I'm just trying to say that if this isn't the most romantic moment, well, I tried. But I see that helping you keep your sanity is the most important thing right now." With those words, Bryan slid off the couch and onto one knee.

Onto one knee?!

What in heaven's name was the man doing?

He'd already proposed. They'd already been married. Heck, they were technically still married. Kenzie's thoughts ran a million miles an hour as Bryan stuck his hand into his pocket and pulled out a gorgeous black velvet box.

Kenzie wiped her hands on her pants, unsure of what else to do. This was definitely not what she'd been expecting. She just wanted Bryan to move back in.

"Kenzie Grace," Bryan said as he took one of Kenzie's sweaty hands. Her left hand.

"What are you doing?" Kenzie blurted at maybe the most inopportune moment. But they hadn't discussed a second proposal. She had no idea how to react.

"Trying to ask you to stay married to me. But you're kind of interrupting," Bryan said in his good-natured way.

Kenzie snapped her lips shut. He was proposing. And this was so sweet. But why? Did it matter? No. She wasn't great with surprises. She liked them but she always figured them out so to be blindsided like this . . .

Wait, Bryan was speaking again and she was missing it.

"I took you for granted," Bryan said.

Kenzie began shaking her head. She was the one who'd taken him for granted.

"Is this your proposal or mine?" Bryan said with a chuckle, as if he hadn't expected anything else from his wife. He was a smart man, so he probably hadn't.

"Yours. Totally yours, but I was the one who took you for granted," Kenzie had to interrupt.

"So when you're saying adoring things to me, go ahead and add that in. But for now . . ."

"Your turn," Kenzie acknowledged, waving her free hand to indicate that Bryan had the floor.

"I love that you take charge. You never take no for an answer, even if it drives me crazy. I love that you pick up my dirty towels from the floor and never utter a word of complaint."

He'd noticed? Kenzie had never thought he did. She'd wondered if he believed in some magic towel fairy who came through their bathroom each morning, but apparently he'd noticed. And she was grateful.

"I love you so completely that even the thought of not being with you for the rest of my life ripped me apart. Changed me into a man I didn't like, one I couldn't face in the mirror. It is only with you that I'm the man I ought to be. It is only because of you that I know the man I can one day be. Kenzie, will you remarry me?" Bryan asked. He opened the box and revealed the most gorgeous oval-cut diamond Kenzie had ever seen in her life. The single stone glimmered even under the terrible lighting in her living room. It rested on a thin white gold band that made the giant rock appear even larger.

But what did remarrying mean? Did he imagine . . .

Kenzie halted the mental hamster wheel mid-spin. She didn't care. For once she was going to jump into something without insisting on all the details first. This was what Bryan wanted and undoubtedly he was doing it because he thought she wanted it too. So she was going to take this blind step and trust her husband. Would he become her re-husband?

No more questions.

"Yes." The word burst out of her.

The pride in Bryan's smile was impossible to miss.

He slipped the ring on her finger and stood, gathering her in his arms as he did so.

"I love you," Bryan uttered as he claimed her lips in a way he hadn't before. Or maybe it was foreign to Kenzie because she was letting him take the lead. Letting herself see where he would take them.

His hands dropped to her waist, tugging Kenzie toward him in an impatient way she was absolutely digging. Her arms wrapped around his neck, eager to tell him she was right there with him. She wanted this. She wanted him. She wanted their forever.

And with just as much force as he'd started the kiss, Bryan pulled away. Kenzie had to admit this side of him was pretty danged hot. Maybe she should give up control a little more often.

"So aren't you going to ask what I mean by remarrying you?" Bryan asked the question that had been tormenting Kenzie, his eyes dancing.

She thought about saying yes, but that could come later. Tonight she'd revealed a new side of herself and Bryan had shown her a new side as well. She was enjoying this all too much to ruin it. Even if she really, really wanted to know what Bryan meant. Was he moving in tomorrow? Next week?

Who knew? But Kenzie could wait. She would wait.

"I think I'd prefer if you went back to kissing me." She surprised herself with the way she practically hummed the words.

With a smirk and then a growl Bryan pulled her in somehow even closer, their bodies nearly one, and did just that.

CHAPTER FIVE

"WE CAN LEAVE if you're exhausted," Callie said to Hazel, seeing that only the five Rosebud girls remained in her living room.

Hazel's parents had insisted on throwing a party for her.

Balloons that spelled out ConGraduation hung on the walls and Hazel had joked that it was her parents' way of dealing with the fact that their only daughter's life had hung in the balance. No one had laughed at the joke. They'd all felt the same.

Although the balloons were kind of a weird choice, Laurel was grateful that at least they didn't spell out the word 'cancer,' even if it had been just to say *you beat cancer* or something equally silly. They'd already lived through it, and no one needed the spelled-out word as a reminder. They were moving on.

Hazel was in the armchair Wells had bought for her as a ConGraduation gift. The thing was state of the art, practically folding out into a bed if desired, but it also had multiple positions between lying down and sitting up. Hazel called it an eyesore, but that hadn't stopped her from asking for it to be placed right next to her couch and then using it for most of the evening. Not that Laurel blamed her. They'd all wondered if the party was too soon, considering how wiped out Hazel had been after each treatment, but her parents had insisted.

That was probably the reason Hazel had told her parents and their friends that the party was over, while insisting that her friends stay to help clean up. As soon as Hazel's parents had left, she had ordered her friends to stop cleaning—Wells had hired a crew to come in the morning—and to relax with her in her living room.

"No way," Hazel replied to Callie's suggestion, even though her eyes were closed. "I feel like I haven't spoken to any of you in forever. I need you all to stay and fill me in on all the gossip I've missed."

"I love you, Hazel, but I'll only share gossip as long as the walls don't have ears. What about your boys?" Callie asked. She craned her neck to peer beyond the kitchen, toward the hall.

"They're set up in some video game tournament. We'll be lucky if we see them before morning," Hazel replied, a soft smile on her face. It was easy to see the contentment she felt when she thought about her boys. So many parts of her life must have felt so uncertain. Laurel could only imagine how reassuring it had been to have her family's unwavering support throughout.

Not that Laurel didn't have family support. Her children were constantly texting to ask how they could help. Both boys had helped her move into her new place, although they had spent much of the time complaining about the neighborhood, and Mari had come over more recently with a ton of house-warming gifts, mostly things from her own apartment that she no longer needed. It was weird to be getting hand-me-downs from her kids. But at the moment that was Laurel's place in life.

"So who's going to start?" Hazel asked. "I know you all have juiciness to share."

Laurel glanced toward Callie, who looked to Kenzie, and then they all turned their attention to Saffron.

"How about you, Hazel?" Saffron asked, a shadow crossing her face as she attempted to deflect the attention from herself.

"What about me?" Hazel replied evasively.

"You look like you're about to fall asleep. You dish first and that way you can't make the excuse that you need to rest when it's your turn later," Saffron said.

Callie and Laurel nodded as Kenzie murmured her assent.

"Looks like we've voted; you're first," Saffron added.

Hazel groaned as she opened her eyes. "Are you really going to make the woman with cancer spill her guts?"

"Are you really going to pull the cancer card?" Kenzie retorted with a sassy tilt of her head.

"Hm," Hazel harrumphed before adjusting her seat to sit up a little straighter.

She looked much less tired now, probably because her parents were gone. Hazel loved the pair and they adored her, but they tended to forget that their daughter was a grown woman with opinions that should be heard, not talked over. It seemed that Hazel never got her way where her parents were concerned, and Laurel imagined that had to be exhausting when she wasn't feeling a hundred percent.

"I don't know what I can tell you. My life is pretty much an open book. You all know I finished chemo last week," Hazel said, spreading her arms as if to show just how open she was.

"Yeah. Total open book. We totally know why your ex-husband is still living with you even though your chemo treatments ended last week. And we also know exactly how you feel about him as well as the gorgeous man who practically lives here even though you've made no kind of commitment to him. Why are we wasting time on you?" Saffron's sarcasm was so thick it could have made a good blanket. Uncomfortable, but thick.

Hazel glared at her friend and then shrugged, dropping her eyes. "Your speculation on that one is as good as mine."

"Liar," Callie accused.

Laurel had to agree but didn't want to gang up on Hazel.

"I honestly don't know why Wells is still here. I've been very vocal about the fact that we are just friends and we have no future together other than as the parents of our boys. I'm guessing he'll be leaving soon? Or maybe he'll stick around until Chase graduates? Who knows?" Hazel sighed and slid down a little further in her chair.

"And Dylan?" Kenzie pressed.

"Can't you let it go?" Hazel groaned.

"No," all four chorused in unison. So much for not ganging up on her, but Laurel couldn't help her instinctive response.

Hazel sighed. "I like him. A lot. I realized I didn't just push him away because I was sick, but also because I was scared. I'm not the woman I was before all of this happened." Her voice was quiet.

Laurel knew they'd have to treat this revelation with kid gloves. This was Hazel's heart.

"Of course you aren't the same woman," she said when no one else spoke. "You are a bad A who has kicked cancer's butt all while maintaining the most important relationships in your life and parenting two of the greatest kids on the planet."

The other three nodded as Hazel watched Laurel, looking hesitant to accept the praise.

"You know I'm right," Laurel pressed. She wasn't typically so forceful but it was important for Hazel to know how incredible she was. She might have lost her hair and a few of her curves, but she was still gorgeous. So gorgeous that Laurel had noticed both Dylan and Wells struggling to keep from staring at her all evening long.

"I did my best. I survived." Hazel admitted only that much.

"You are magnificent in every way. Still the most beautiful girl in the room," Callie said meaningfully.

"Now I know you're lying," Hazel replied hastily, as if she couldn't even listen to such a preposterous notion.

"She's not at all," Saffron retorted.

Hazel scoffed and Saffron jumped to her feet, striding across the room.

"What are you doing?" Kenzie asked.

"Hazel needs to see this," Saffron said, lifting a circular mirror from the kitchen wall. She brought it to Hazel and held it up in front of her face.

"I already know what I look like," Hazel said softly, her eyes averted.

"No, really look," Saffron insisted.

Hazel's gaze had been flitting around the room, glancing at anything but the mirror, but with a grimace she stared dead ahead.

"Happy?" she asked as her eyes bored into her reflection.

"What do you see?" Saffron prodded.

"A really skinny, pale woman with a scarf covering her head," Hazel said. She gently pushed the mirror aside, tilting it so she could no longer see herself.

"How many people complimented you on that scarf?" Saffron asked.

"They just felt sorry for me. That was better than 'sorry you have to cover up the fact that you lost all your hair,'" Hazel replied feistily.

"Or maybe they really liked the scarf. I know I do. It goes perfectly with your eyes. Even though chemo has ravaged your body, you somehow look younger than when you started. You practically glow with happiness now that you're done." While Saffron spoke the others watched silently, fervently hoping her words would get through. Hazel deserved to know how beautiful she was. More than ever, she needed that confidence.

"And many women would pay thousands to have your figure as it is right now. I know I would," Callie stated.

Laurel nodded her agreement. Hazel was a little skinnier than she'd been before, but she still had the booty that had won 'nicest behind' in high school. It had been a student-run hoss election, unbeknownst to the teachers, and as an adult Laurel now found it to be a terrible thing for a teen's self-esteem. But she still remembered the day Hazel had won, thinking it was well deserved.

"You guys are my friends. You have to say that," Hazel said. She pushed against the mirror again, a little harder this time.

"You're right," Laurel said. "And as your friends it is our duty to make sure that you see yourself—really see yourself."

"So that's all that's keeping you away from Dylan?" Kenzie asked, looking like she'd had her fill of the sappy talk. She was always ready to get down to business.

Hazel shrugged as if ashamed that it was the only reason.

"That man worships the ground you walk on," Kenzie said, pausing until Hazel met her eyes. "You've spent the last five months fighting for your life. Now how about you spend the next five months fighting to live that life the way you want? Because you want Dylan. I see it in your eyes. So go get him," Kenzie said in her typical brusque manner. Only she could make something that had felt impossible just moments before look like the easiest thing in the world.

"What if I tell him how I feel and then he stays with me because he feels sorry for me?" Hazel bit her lip as she revealed her fear.

"That wouldn't be the reason," Callie said confidently.

"You can't know that," Hazel replied.

She was right. They couldn't know anything, not for sure.

But Dylan would be a fool if he couldn't see Hazel for who she was, if he'd lost his love for her because she'd been battling cancer. And Laurel knew that Dylan was no fool.

"You told him you don't want to date him and he's still here. You've basically pitted him against your ex and he's held his ground," Saffron retorted.

"I have not," Hazel protested weakly as Saffron continued.

"Fine. Give it another week, two weeks, five months. However long it takes to see that Dylan isn't around because he pities you. Your hair will start growing back and your bum will regain all of its former glory. Then will you finally tell him how you feel? Is it worth losing all this time you could have had with a man who loves you, just for your pride?" Saffron asked the hard questions.

Hazel flinched. But she was obviously taking it in. Laurel was sure Saffron's words had found their mark and she hoped it would cause Hazel to make her move. Dylan deserved her and she deserved him, and Laurel thought it was about time they acted on it.

"Speaking of letting your pride get in the way, I heard you not only let your amazing sous go without a fight, but you shoved him out, not allowing him his final two weeks." Callie seemed to understand that Hazel needed time to process, so she turned to Saffron —who all of a sudden had to leave the room to return the mirror to its place.

"You aren't getting away," Kenzie called after her.

"There's really nothing to dig into there. Alex wanted a new job. He found one. End of story," Saffron called behind her as she rehung the mirror, her back turned to her friends.

"Didn't he need to work at the Lodge because he wanted to stay close to his mom?" Kenzie asked.

"Mario's head chef quit on him and Alex was there at the right time," Saffron explained, referring to the upscale Mexican restaurant in the middle of town. It always had a line winding out the door and onto Main Street.

"He's a head chef? That's amazing; Alex deserves that," Laurel said, then clamped her mouth shut as she realized the words might hurt Saffron. But even Saffron had to see that it was a vertical move he couldn't pass up, didn't she?

"He does," Saffron said in a detached voice as she came back to the living room and sat. "And he doesn't have to worry about his mom so much anymore because he has Cherry."

That last word got all of the emotion that Saffron's other words had lacked. She practically spit the name across the room.

"So I take it we don't like Cherry?" Kenzie asked, sliding a little closer to Saffron on the couch they were sharing.

"We love Cherry. Cherry is Alex's choice and we want Alex to be happy," Saffron said, her dead voice now back.

"From what I've heard, Cherry is driving Alex insane, pulling stunts like showing up at his job and throwing a fit worthy of a toddler," Callie replied.

"I don't know why we're still talking about this. Yes, Alex left me in the lurch. But I'll find someone new." Saffron crossed her arms over her chest.

"It would have been less of a lurch if you'd let him work his last two weeks," Kenzie muttered.

Saffron ignored her. "I have Nick. We're covering things fine. I'm looking at applications and we'll have a new hire in the next week or so. We're fine. Everything is fine."

"Sounds fine," Hazel said dryly, causing almost everyone to chuckle.

Saffron just glared.

"And personally? How did Alex's leaving make you feel?" Kenzie softened her voice as she asked the question all of the girls were wondering.

"Personally? Personally?" Saffron's voice reached squeaking

tones. "*Personally*, I want to kick him in the head and ask him what the hell he was thinking dating a woman like Cherry when he knew a woman like me was interested in him."

Saffron sighed. She definitely hadn't meant to say so much. But the pain she'd been storing up had reached the bursting level and just slipped out.

"I'm sorry, Saff," Laurel said when she saw the way her friend's frown covered her entire face. Even her nose looked upset.

Saffron shrugged. "It is what it is."

The other girls shared a look. They'd all expected Alex to make his move long ago, even before Cherry had entered the picture. He'd seemed even more into Saffron than she was into him. But now they wondered. Callie had overheard the argument between Cherry and Alex in the kitchen and had told the others she was sure they'd either broken up or were just about to. It seemed that their relationship had been steadily declining for a long time, so they'd assumed that Alex had taken this new job so that he could finally ask Saffron out. But it had been a few days since he'd quit now, and surely Saffron would have told them if he'd made any sort of move. Maybe they'd all read him wrong?

Kenzie looked the most regretful of them all. Laurel knew that she wouldn't have pushed this conversation if she'd known that Alex had given Saffron no hope for a future. What was the man thinking?

"Riley asked me out," Laurel blurted to relieve the tension and sorrow in the room.

But oh heavens, she was an idiot. All eyes instantly swiveled to her and the frowns vanished. She'd successfully moved their attention away from Saffron's situation. But judging by the smirks and knowing smiles on their faces, maybe she should have said anything but that.

"He did?" Callie squealed, bouncing up and down in her seat.

"He's so hot," Kenzie added, as she fanned her face appreciatively.

"So attractive," Hazel agreed. "Oh, and Dylan told me he's given Riley some ink. I don't know where, but maybe Laurel can find out for us," she added with a pump of her eyebrows.

"He didn't *ask me out* ask me out," Laurel had to clarify.

"What does that even mean?" Kenzie muttered as Saffron spoke over her.

"What were his exact words?" Saffron seemed as invested as the rest of them and for that Laurel was grateful, but she was still kicking herself for bringing this up.

"He said . . . " Laurel paused, pretending she'd forgotten the words that had been playing on repeat in her mind since she'd left Riley's office. But heck she was in for a penny, might as well offer the pound. "He said, 'I'm going to ask you out when you're ready. But I figured I'd give you a head's up. Then maybe you'll be ready sooner.'"

"Ahhh!" Hazel yelped, clasping her hands together as she sat straight up in the still-reclined chair.

"Oh goodness gracious," Callie added.

Saffron beamed and Kenzie just stared.

"He's even hotter now," Kenzie breathed when she was able to speak again.

"So what did you say?" Saffron asked, scooting to the edge of the couch.

"I may have had a mini panic attack and then left?" Laurel admitted almost inaudibly.

Hazel barked out a laugh.

"It's really terrible isn't it?" Laurel whispered, sinking as far back into the couch as she could and vaguely wishing it would just swallow her up.

"Terrible, as in it will make a good story for your grandkids one day, or terrible, as in you think it's going to scare him off? Because honey, the latter isn't happening. The man is smitten, S-M-I-T-T-E-N," Saffron said, her smile now as expansive as her frown had been.

But Laurel couldn't even enjoy Saffron's delight because she was in the middle of freaking out.

"I'm not having kids with him." Laurel's uterus shriveled at the thought. She may not have hit menopause yet but it was coming soon. And one thing her uterus wasn't going to be doing? Popping out any more kids.

"You already have kids, silly," Callie said. "If you marry Riley, they'll be his stepkids and you'll share the grandkids you'll eventually have." Callie stated it as if it were a done deal. But it wasn't. Not even close. She couldn't even say yes to a date.

"Do you think he's thought this through?" Laurel asked as she considered how young Riley seemed compared to her nearly grandma status. Granted, they were the same age, but he was the town's most eligible bachelor. Definitely younger seeming than the mother of three grown children.

"Pretty sure he's been thinking of no one but you for a long time," Callie said softly, as if she knew more than the rest of them.

"Probably too long," Kenzie added. "We all saw that Bennie wasn't treating you the way he should have been. I bet that drove a man with feelings for you right up the wall."

"He didn't have feelings for me then," Laurel said firmly. "I was married."

Callie didn't look so sure. "I've heard rumors that he's liked you for years. That it started as a crush in high school but then he'd compare every woman in his life to you. I always brushed them aside because you had Bennie, but it makes sense."

"That's why he's never dated anyone seriously. He's been pining for our Laurel," Hazel added with a tilt of her head.

"You all are really freaking me out. He has not liked me for that long and there has been no pining. He's just been spending a lot of time with me because he's helping me and the close proximity has forced him to think that maybe he should ask me out. When he really shouldn't. He should be looking for a woman who can give him kids." Laurel's train of thought was derailing despite her efforts to keep it on track.

"He wants kids?" Saffron asked.

"How should I know?" Laurel threw her hands in the air in an very un-Laurel-like manner.

"Laurel is losing it. I say we move on to other highly attractive men. Like Leo." Hazel's eyebrows were getting a workout with how often she kept pumping them.

Was Riley really into her? Laurel had been sure it was pity that led him to ask her out. Well, not sure. His words had been so sincere and—her friends were right—hot, but it just made no sense. She and Riley. Riley and Laurel.

But did she want him asking out anyone else?

Laurel knew the answer to that in her core. Hell no. Sometime between his almost asking her out and today Laurel's heart had laid claim to Riley, whether he liked it or not. Oh shoot, she liked him. What was she supposed to do now? She hadn't dated a new man since Bennie, nearly thirty years before.

"Leo and I are taking a break," Callie said, startling Laurel out of her confused thoughts.

Kenzie gasped and quickly covered her mouth.

"I'm so sorry," Hazel replied immediately.

Saffron and Laurel sat staring at Callie with wide eyes.

None of them had had any idea.

"He doesn't want to get married . . . ever. And you all know how I feel about marriage." Callie tried to keep her voice light but Laurel could see that her eyes were getting red around the rims, a sure sign that she was about to cry. How had Callie kept this from them? And why?

"I just . . . I can't talk about it yet. Can we move on, please?" Callie asked in a strained voice. She glanced at Kenzie. "In fact, Kenzie has some news."

"Here? Now?" Kenzie asked, looking from Callie to Hazel and then back to Callie.

"Why not? The party is over. We're all sharing news," Callie said, blinking and manufacturing a bright smile. Kenzie seemed to acknowledge this and reached into her pocket, bringing out the blingiest ring Laurel had ever seen.

"Bryan reproposed. We're getting remarried and I don't even know what that means," Kenzie announced with a shy smile.

The room was silent for a moment.

Kenzie didn't know what it meant, yet she was doing it? Laurel was confused.

"So, like a vow renewal?" Hazel asked.

"Who knows?" Kenzie said excitedly. "But Bryan wants to do this right before he moves back in with me."

Laurel felt a smile spread over her face. She couldn't be any happier for her friend. Kenzie using a phrase like 'who knows' was foreign, but if it made her that blissful it must be right.

"Where is Bryan tonight?" Saffron wondered.

"I wanted to keep it under wraps since this party was about Hazel, so I told him I'd see him later tonight," Kenzie said.

"Later tonight? That's so college Kenzie of you," Callie teased.

"Right?" Kenzie giggled excitedly.

"So you've been hiding that gorgeous thing in your pocket all night?" Hazel asked. "You love me more than I love you. I wouldn't have been able to keep that stunner to myself."

Kenzie laughed again, with Saffron, Callie, and Laurel soon joining her.

"Wait, how did Callie know?" Saffron asked.

"She saw the outline of the ring in my pocket," Kenzie said dryly.

Laurel shook her head fondly. Leave it to Callie to notice something like that.

"Ah!" Saffron squealed and Laurel understood. She wasn't sure how to deal with all she was feeling either.

"So when is the big day?" Laurel asked.

"I have no idea," Kenzie said, her voice getting a little too high.

"Maybe you should have a talk with Bryan?" Callie suggested.

"Yeah, I probably should. But we've been a little too busy kissing to do much talking," Kenzie admitted, her cheeks burning red.

"Totally college Kenz," Saffron joked.

It was. But Laurel was glad to see it. It was about time Kenzie let some things go.

"But what I do know is that I want the four of you by my side at whatever a remarriage is," Kenzie said as she met the eyes of each of her friends.

"We wouldn't miss it for the world," Laurel promised.

The others nodded their agreement. No matter what was going on in each of their own lives, when one girl celebrated or mourned, the rest would as well. It was what they did.

CHAPTER SIX

HAZEL SAT on the edge of her bed, ready to get up after her nap. It had been a blessed week since she'd felt any chemo side effects and every day symptom-free had her in good spirits. After feeling lousy for so long it felt incredible to just feel okay.

She smiled to herself as she stood up, listening to the sounds of the house around her. She heard the washing machine, which meant the cleaning woman Wells had hired was hard at work. The tv was on in the living room, probably a baseball game Wells couldn't miss. Chase called out to his brother and then Wells yelled just as loudly to keep it down so that Hazel could sleep. She smiled. She loved her dysfunctional little family.

Hazel had fallen into a routine of daily naps that would ordinarily horrify her, but since she had been kicking cancer's butt she figured she could give herself a pass. It seemed everyone else was doing so too.

Her ex was here keeping everything in the house in check, her boys had somehow behaved for nearly five months straight, and then there was Dylan. Dylan had been her lifeline to the world, the buoy she'd clung to during the storm. If Wells had been the one to keep the day-to-day of Hazel's home running,

Dylan had been the one to keep Hazel running. He'd literally helped her stand on the days she'd been too weak to do so on her own, figured out that the only thing Hazel could eat at her most nauseated was watermelon with Tajin, and had stayed late into the night on those first days after chemo when Hazel felt so hollowed out by her treatments that she worried she wouldn't wake up the next morning. With Dylan's assurance that she would, she'd finally fall asleep. And he'd quietly leave at who knew what hour to get the tiniest bits of sleep before getting up for work the next morning.

Hazel moved to stand in front of her mirror, wincing at her bald head, saggy face, and just as saggy bum on full display in her barely-there pajamas. She critically took in the sallowness of her skin, the dullness of her eyes, and the drooping of her boobs. Hazel had known aging would be hard for a woman like her who'd always been valued for her looks, who had always seen her own value in her looks. She knew it hadn't been healthy and now she was reaping the fruits of those values. Not only was she aging, but she was doing it at an accelerated pace thanks to cancer and chemo, her two least favorite c-words.

Is this what Dylan saw? How could he love her?

Even as she doubted, Hazel heard a voice in her mind that sounded a lot like Saffron: wasn't what Dylan had done for her the actions of a man in love? Just because Hazel was too shallow to see beyond her looks to her actual worth, it didn't mean Dylan was the same.

Was Hazel not giving him enough credit? Saffron would answer that with a resounding hell yes.

But weren't men visually spurred into relationships? That's what Hazel had always been taught. Men had to be physically attracted to their partners. Women found things like humor, drive, or even money equally attractive. But a man needed to think his woman was beautiful, or it just didn't work.

And there was no way any man could think this mess she faced in the mirror was attractive.

But Dylan wasn't any man. He was the man who'd continued to stand by her even as she had literally deteriorated. He had been in love with her before all of this. Did she expect his love to just dissipate along with her looks? Did she really think him that shallow? She considered what would have happened had the situation been reversed. If Hazel had loved Dylan but he'd been diagnosed with cancer, could she have walked away because he didn't look the same?

She felt sick at the very thought.

And heaven knew Dylan would have probably still have looked sexy through chemo. If any man could, it would have been Dylan.

So if she wouldn't have walked away, if her love for Dylan wouldn't have changed, couldn't it be that he was still in love with her? Maybe he was just waiting for Hazel to be ready to let him love her. Was she really wasting time that she could spend with a man as incredible as Dylan, putting him on hold, hoping her looks would come back, just for her pride?

Hell yes! Again her inner voice sounded a lot like Saffron.

So what are you going to do about it? Inner Saffron asked.

Hazel really needed to get ahold of her inner voice and reprogram it. Saffron would be way too cocky if she ever heard how she'd become Hazel's conscience.

But what was Hazel going to do about it?

She met her eyes in the mirror and suddenly an entire plan came to her mind.

———

"MOM?" Chase asked as Hazel emerged from her bathroom several hours later.

She'd gone all out. She'd self-tanned to counteract her sallow skin. She'd hydrated and then masked up with all of the makeup she could get her hands on. She'd even brought out the wig that most closely resembled her do before chemo had taken it all from her, although the wig did itch like the dickens. She wore a pair of jeans that made her feel confident and a top that did its best to buoy up those drooping breasts. Under her jeans she'd even shaved her legs. All that work in her chemo-weakened state had exhausted her. But she looked better than she had in months.

Hazel was back.

"What do you think?" she asked Chase. She thought about attempting a twirl but thought she might pass out if she did so. Instead she waved her hands over her figure.

"You look like a knock-out, Mom," Chase said, eyeing her warily. "But you are gorgeous without all of that too. You know that, right?"

Wait, even her eighteen-year-old knew this was just an attempt to cover up her insecurities? When had he become so intuitive? And how could she make him stop? Hazel felt her heart stutter. She really hoped Dylan wouldn't see through her the same way Chase had. The last thing she wanted was for Dylan to feel pity for her.

A whistle sounded from behind Hazel and she spun toward the noise, immediately grateful she hadn't twirled for Chase earlier. Judging by the fact that the half spin left her swaying, a full spin would have landed her on her saggy, not-as-padded bottom.

"You look amazing," Wells said as he appreciatively took in his ex-wife.

"Cut it out," Hazel said even as she reveled in the praise. This was the woman she'd once been. A woman who could make her ex eat his heart out with a single glance. A woman who could win over the heart of the best man she ever knew.

"Can't help it. I'm just speaking the truth," Wells said with a wink before turning back to his baseball game, once again oblivious to anything else.

And now she remembered exactly what it was like to be married to him.

"I thought I heard Dylan come in?" Hazel turned to Chase, who was making a sandwich in the kitchen.

"He's downstairs with Sterling. Something about a rematch from last weekend," Chase said, biting down into the enormous food item in his hands. He had to have nearly an entire package of deli meat between those two pieces of bread.

Hazel fought the urge to groan. Those video game matches could take hours.

And judging by the empty boxes of pizza all over her kitchen countertop, they'd taken dinner down with them, so they had enough sustenance to last the duration. Hazel really wasn't going to see Dylan tonight. After all this effort.

"Didn't you just have pizza?" Hazel asked as Chase chewed hungrily. She focused her attention on him instead of on the fact that her plan had flopped big time. Maybe she shouldn't have shaved her legs; she might have been out in time.

She scratched at the incessant itching on her scalp. Stupid wig.

"Dad only ordered four pies," Chase shrugged as he took a second bite of his gigantic sandwich. It was so big Hazel felt that she should name it.

"Silly me, thinking an entire large pizza was enough food for a single person," Wells said, his eyes never leaving the tv.

"We have five people and four pies, Dad," Chase said around his mouthful.

"We saved two pieces for Mom. From my pizza."

Hazel didn't have to see Wells' face to know he was rolling his eyes. Even the back of his head told Hazel he wasn't amused.

"So I only got my one pizza. Anyway, long story short, Mom, I'm still hungry." Chase flipped his hair out of his eyes.

After her boys had shaved their heads for her, Hazel had worried that their hair would grow back oddly or at least not as beautiful as it had once been, but both now had manes they were somehow even more proud of. That was saying something, considering both of her boys had always been a little vain when it came to their hair. Like mother, like sons.

Chase's blonde hair had come back in a little lighter than before and with even more of a wave, giving it volume for days. Sterling's hair had grown back the same color as his pre-shaved head, but like Chase, his also now had some wave to it and both loved flipping and flopping their hair this way and that.

Hazel couldn't help but wonder what her hair would look like one day. Would it come back completely gray? With how much she'd had to color it the past few years to hide her increasing supply of silver strands, Hazel wouldn't be surprised. Ugh. Cancer sucked.

"You could always go strut yourself down there," Chase offered.

"I'm not strutting anywhere," Hazel said indignantly, folding her arms across her chest.

"Didn't say you were." Chase raised his hands in surrender momentarily before returning to his sandwich.

"I'll say it for you, then. Hazel, you were totally strutting your stuff. And I appreciate it, doll," Wells said, his eyes still fixed on the screen rather than on her.

If she hadn't already been so sure of her decision to choose Dylan over Wells, this would have made it a done deal. Granted, Wells hadn't voiced a desire to have Hazel back for a couple of months now. Maybe it was all a thing of the past. She hoped so. As much as she enjoyed giving Wells a hard time, she still felt a deep affection for him—just not the romantic kind—and she would hate to see him actually hurt by her choosing Dylan.

"She isn't doing it for you, Dad," Chase pointed out.

"I'm all too aware of that, son. But thank you," Wells said before yelling, "He was totally safe!"

Good. Wells wasn't going to be hurt. He understood she was choosing Dylan. In fact, it almost seemed as if he wanted her to choose Dylan. Hazel felt relief that she and Wells were on the same page. They worked well as friends and coparents, terribly as a married couple.

But what was not so good? Dylan being downstairs with Sterling for who knew how long.

"So does this mean you're finally going to put Dylan out of his misery?" Chase asked, cramming the last bite of his sandwich into his mouth. Still chewing, he opened the fridge and began to rummage through the contents. Feeding teenaged boys was no joke.

"What do you mean?" Hazel attempted to play dumb but realized this was her son. She should have just deflected instead. If she'd brought up school or girls he would have forgotten his question.

"I know that you know Dylan is crazy about you. For months now he's been hoping to be your official boyfriend. Although why he wants to tie himself down to one woman when he could have dozens I'll never understand." Chase pulled out a two-liter bottle of soda and was about to chug it straight from the container.

"Glass," Hazel warned.

Chase sighed, trudging the whole five steps to get a glass and fill it up rather than contaminating the bottle everyone shared with backwash.

"Exactly!" Wells concurred from the living room a few seconds too late.

What was Wells agreeing to? What had Chase been saying? Oh, right. Dylan wanting her and only her. Dylan didn't want to date dozens of women, but her son had glorified that option.

She needed to address that first.

"Chase. You do realize the whole point of dating is to find one right woman for you. One you can share a life with," Hazel said, hating that Chase had watched his dad spend months doing the exact opposite of what she was trying to promote.

"Like you and Dad found?" Chase asked.

"Touché," Wells called out.

Hazel fought the urge to throw something at the back of his fat head.

"Your dad and I were happy for years and we have two beautiful boys, thanks to our time together."

"What she's trying to say is that we didn't completely waste the twenty years we were together. I barely realized what I was missing out on—until I was finally single again." Wells threw in his two cents with a smirk, which Chase returned.

"Wells. Stop 'helping,'" Hazel ground out.

She saw him shrug his big shoulders and hoped that meant he was out of this conversation for good.

"I get it, Mom," Chase said before Hazel could go on. "And if I find that woman worth ignoring all of the other girls for, great. But until then, I'm going to have a lot of fun searching."

He flashed his charming grin at her.

Hazel just shook her head. Boys.

"Just make sure you're the kind of guy worthy of that woman you're looking for," Hazel said with a pointed nod of her head.

"Mom, have you looked at me? Definitely worthy," Chase said. He set his empty glass in the sink and flexed his bicep.

Hallelujah, he was finally learning. About the glass, that is. Hazel had spent at least a month of her life gathering cups from around the house. She pulled her mind back to the conversation. Chase had said something stupid.

"Chase," Hazel warned.

"What?" he responded too innocently.

Hazel was worried about that tone, but she was more concerned with what her son thought.

"Do you really think as long as you're handsome that's all you have to bring to the table?" she asked.

"Wait, you're telling me other things matter more than looks?"

"Everything matters more than looks," Hazel exclaimed, raising her hands in the air.

"I know," Chase said, propping his elbows on the counter and leaning across it toward his mom. "And that's why even though Dylan is going to be blown away by how gorgeous you look tonight, you didn't have to do it. He thinks you look just as amazing in your sweats and without that itchy wig. Because he loves you."

Hazel dropped her hands, her mouth wide open.

"This was all just a trap?" she asked over Wells' laughter.

She would deal with him later.

"Not just a trap. But a lesson," Chase said. Hazel could've sworn she'd once said the exact same words to him. She hated these turning tables.

But even as she bubbled with frustration, pride welled within her. Her boys were listening and learning. They understood what she'd been trying to teach them. Now if only she could get it through her own thick skull as well.

She knew looks didn't truly matter. If anyone else had had cancer and lost so much of their former physical beauty, Hazel would have surely found a new list of beautiful things about them. And not just on the inside either. She would have seen an outer beauty in these others that she just couldn't find in herself.

And she hated that. Because if anyone deserved her love, wasn't it herself?

"So the student becomes the teacher?" Hazel asked, admitting defeat.

Chase rounded the counter and lightly put his arm around Hazel's shoulders. "Nope. I'll always be the student because my mama is much wiser than I am."

"Can I get that in writing?" Hazel asked.

"Not a chance," Chase responded without missing a beat. "But my stunning mama needed a reminder tonight. That although she is still as pretty as she's ever been . . . "

Hazel opened her mouth.

"Don't you dare contradict me while I'm trying to have a moment," Chase said with a tsk, one eyebrow raised warningly.

Hazel was sure she'd said that once or a dozen times as well.

"The man who loves her sees so much more than that. Love isn't being so blinded by outer beauty that you put up with what's on the inside. Love is a connection between two people, such an incredible bond that you can't see where they end and you begin. Love isn't seeing through rose-colored glasses. Love makes the world rose colored."

Hazel's mouth dropped open once again. Who was this young man and what had he done with her immature son?

"If he's half the man I think he is, you telling him you're ready to love him back is everything he could ever want. Because his world will be complete. Not because you look good in a pair of tight jeans."

"She looks hot." Wells added his unnecessary commentary once again.

Chase frowned.

"Hearing my dad call my mom, who happens to be his ex-wife, hot isn't weird at all," Chase said as he dropped his arm from Hazel's shoulders.

"Just telling it like it is," Wells said before throwing the remote on the couch. "That pitch was a strike. Right down the middle!"

"With that, I'm off on my own adventures," Chase said with a shake of his head.

"Chase, thank you," Hazel managed, her emotions surging powerfully. "I don't know when you became so astute but I am so, so grateful to have you as a son. You make me proud, kid."

She gently slugged him on the shoulder instead of hugging him, since she'd watched his face transform from pride to discomfort in just a few seconds of her rambling. Her boys never had done well with excessive praise.

Chase suddenly grinned. "Wait, am I so astute that I don't have to have a curfew, because you trust me to make those kinds of decisions for myself?"

"I think you're so astute that you know exactly what my answer to that question will be," Hazel replied with a wink.

Chase groaned.

"In four months you'll be at Vanderbilt. Your no-curfew days are in the very near future, and because of your astuteness tonight I feel a little less wary about those days," Hazel added.

Chase smiled. "Vanderbilt. Four months." He said the words wistfully.

Hazel laughed. She was going to miss this boy.

On that note, Chase jogged out toward the garage and it was just her and Wells. Or her and Wells and the game.

"He's right, you know," Wells said, his eyes glued to the game.

"Were you even listening?" Hazel asked, her hands on her hips. Somehow almost every conversation with Wells ended with her hands on her hips.

"I heard enough. Did you know I wasn't even attracted to you when I first met you?" Wells asked.

Hazel scoffed. Wells had literally written songs about how her golden hair had drawn him from across the crowd.

"Okay, let me amend that. I wasn't more attracted to you than I was to plenty of other women. There are hundreds of thousands of Hazels around the world if your looks are the only factor."

Hazel cocked her head. She wasn't sure if she should be offended or grateful. Where was he going with this?

"Do you remember what you said when I asked you for your number?" Wells asked.

"I told you that you could give me yours, and we'd see if I got around to calling you," Hazel recalled. Those words had also been immortalized in one of his songs.

Wells chuckled. "You cast your hook. And you totally caught me with those words. And then do you remember our first date?"

"You made the waitress cry?" Hazel asked.

Wells finally turned away from the game at that accusation.

"How was I supposed to know she'd be working there?" he tried to defend himself.

"Oh, I don't know. Maybe if you had called her back after your one date with her you would have known." Hazel smirked.

"I went on just one date with dozens of girls before that. None of them reacted that way to seeing me again," Wells said, his eyes drifting back toward the tv.

"Did you ever see any of them again?"

Wells didn't respond, which gave Hazel the answer.

"Anyway, you comforted our waitress, made sure she kept her job even as she was sobbing, and then left me because, and let me get this quote right, 'I was a douchebag.'"

"You were," Hazel said, shrugging a shoulder that Wells wouldn't see because the douchebag was watching the game.

"I'd never seen a woman treat a complete stranger with such kindness. I had to go out with you again. I knew you were the one."

"You did not," Hazel replied quickly.

There was also a song about the moment Wells had fallen in love with her. The timeline of their relationship was worldwide knowledge.

"I did. The bar where you danced like no one was watching was when I knew I had to marry you immediately, but after that first date I was already in love. But it wasn't because you were gorgeous. You were, and you still are. But I fell in love because you're you. And although Dylan is an idiot, even he can see that. He might actually be the one of us smart enough to never let you go."

That may have been the sweetest thing Wells had ever said to her. And it only took marriage, a few rocky years, divorce, and then cancer to get it out of him. But Hazel was touched nonetheless, although she wasn't about to tell him that. It would only cause his head to inflate even more. So she stuck with what she did best: teasing Wells.

"So Dylan isn't an idiot then," Hazel said with a grin.

"Oh, he is. It's just that I'm an even bigger one," Wells admitted to the tv.

Hazel wouldn't disagree with that. But even if he was an idiot, Hazel couldn't help loving the man who'd given her twenty happy years. Okay, maybe more like eighteen because those last two had been rough.

"All of that." Wells looked at her again, this time waving a hand up and down over the length of Hazel. "It's just the pretty polish. Sure, it adds to the shine, but it isn't what makes you shine. It isn't what draws us in."

The moment he finished those sweet words, Wells was right back to the game. And Hazel was glad. She wasn't quite sure how to react.

"Thanks, Wells," she finally said. The words didn't feel sufficient, but she wasn't sure what would be.

"Don't mention it. Like, seriously don't. I'm guessing I'll finally find another woman who I'm willing to spend the next twenty years with and she will never be hearing about this conversation," Wells said, managing the whole comment without missing a second of the game.

Hazel grinned, feeling happy for Wells that he was ready to settle down again, but a little pity for the woman he chose. She hoped the future Mrs. Wells liked baseball.

Hazel, high on the words of her son and ex, decided that they were right. Saffron, the girls, Wells, Chase—they were all right, and she'd been wrong. She'd not only underestimated Dylan, but she'd underestimated herself.

She returned to the bathroom. Thankfully all of the stuff on her face was much easier to remove than apply. She was back in another set of pajamas and tucked into bed with a romance novel when she heard Dylan's signature knock on her door hours later.

"That must have been quite the match-up," Hazel said, closing her book and patting the bed beside her.

Dylan's big body caused the bed to sink and Hazel found herself rolling into his side, just the place she wanted to be.

"I would steer clear of Sterling for a bit. I kept winning and he kept asking for rematches. I finally threw the last game and I know he suspects it, but I hope you'll forgive me for lying to your son."

"Lies of survival. We all tell them," Hazel said, only able to joke about it because she knew Dylan loved her boys nearly as much as she did. He'd never lie if it would actually hurt either of them.

"I missed you tonight, though," Dylan said. He wrapped a strong arm around Hazel, pulling her even closer to him.

"I missed you too," she admitted. She hadn't spoken those words aloud in a long time because she'd been trying so hard to push Dylan away.

"Did you?" Dylan asked.

"I always do," Hazel said.

Dylan dropped a kiss on the top of her head and she was so content she nearly purred.

Then, without thinking, she reciprocated Dylan's kiss, pressing her lips to his shoulder.

She felt his body tense beside her.

"Is everything okay?" he asked, his voice laced with concern.

She hoped so. She hoped what she was about to give him was good news. She was pretty sure it was going to be. But even her slight doubt wasn't going to stop her now. She felt slightly less confident now that she was no longer in her mask of false beauty, but this felt right. Barefaced, bareheaded, in pajamas: it was the way she'd seen Dylan so many times. It was the way she wanted Dylan to accept her. So this look made sense.

And now that she'd finally learned that she had more to offer the world and a man than just her looks, she wasn't going to let anything stop her. She was allowing her love for herself to grow enough to pursue him. And if he didn't love her, she'd deal with that later.

"I've been thinking," Hazel began. "I'm done with chemo."

"Thank heavens," Dylan muttered before kissing her head again.

"I still don't know how the chips will fall. I won't officially be cancer-free for years," Hazel continued.

"I know," was all Dylan said, giving her his full attention as he waited for her to speak in her own time.

"I'm sure this has to be difficult for you. I don't want to live with this uncertainty but I have to. I need you to know that you can still get out. You can go." Hazel was giving him an easy out. What was she doing? She was supposed to be doing the opposite of this. But she felt it was only fair. The last thing she wanted to do was trap Dylan.

"Go where?" he asked, sounding confused.

"Anywhere you want," Hazel said, realizing the world was Dylan's oyster.

"I want," Dylan paused and then dropped his arm from her shoulders as he turned his body to look straight into her eyes. "to be with you. Whether that's in this house, at a hospital, or anywhere in between. It's the only place I want to be."

Hazel felt her heart lift. He really did love her. Still. Despite all of this.

"Okay," Hazel said with a grin.

"I feel like there's a lot behind that 'okay.'"

"There is." Hazel threw a teasing smirk.

"You are driving me wild, woman," Dylan groaned.

"Behind that 'okay' is my truth: I feel the exact same way. With you is the only place I want to be."

"Really?" Dylan pushed up on one elbow and turned to face her, hope filling his voice.

Hazel nodded. "I plan on growing really old with you. So don't think cancer will be getting rid of me."

Dylan chuckled. "If anyone could scare cancer, it would be you."

"That's right," Hazel said, her energy building so much that she had to rise to her knees. "I love you, Dylan." She breathed the words and held her breath, watching Dylan's reaction.

"I love you more than you could ever know," Dylan replied immediately, as if he didn't even have to think. He just knew.

He gathered Hazel into his arms in the next moment and even as she anticipated what was coming next, nothing could compare to the feeling of Dylan's lips meeting hers.

They were gentle at first, the first touches of a love that was being discovered, and then he pulled her close, claiming her as his in the same breath she was claiming him.

"Is Dylan still here?" Sterling called from just outside Hazel's door. Panicked, she fell against her pillows and covered her head with her blanket, feeling like a teenager caught sneaking out.

Dylan chuckled, apparently not embarrassed in the slightest.

"I hear you in there, Dylan. I know you threw that last game. I need a rematch," Sterling called.

Hazel peeked out from under the blanket just in time to see Dylan's eyes hungrily take her in.

"We'll have to hold that thought. But know that I'll be thinking about little else," he promised.

"You know, if you're planning on becoming the boys' stepdad you'll have to learn how to say no," Hazel teased. She gulped as she realized what she'd just said. They weren't even close to talking about marriage.

Hazel dove under her blanket again.

She felt a gentle tug at the blanket. Her face was unveiled to see Dylan smiling tenderly at her.

"Are you proposing to me, Hazel?" he drawled.

"Nope, never," Hazel stammered.

"Good," Dylan said. "Because I'd love to be the one to propose you. So you'd better be on the lookout. I've never been one to be patient."

With those words Dylan stood, leaving her with one final, longing look as she covered her pounding heart with her hands.

Yeah, she was glad she hadn't waited a week, two weeks, or five months more. Any day spent not loving Dylan was a day wasted.

CHAPTER SEVEN

"THIS IS IT," Kenzie said as she stepped out from behind the curtain in the changing area where Laurel was waiting with both of their purses.

"It's beautiful," Laurel gushed as she took in the blush pink dress that Kenzie wore.

Bryan had finally told her what he imagined a remarriage to be and Kenzie had been fully on board: a small ceremony with just the people they loved most as they renewed their vows, followed by a party with all of those important-to-them people. Simple and easy, but the next step to the rest of their lives. Although he'd insisted on still calling it a remarriage instead of a vow renewal, and he'd told her he would explain it the night before their ceremony. It was sweet and romantic and she couldn't wait.

But because it wouldn't be a traditional ceremony—Bryan and Kenzie would be walking down the aisle together and her dad would be reading their vows of renewal—Kenzie felt that she should wear something other than white.

"The pink works?" she asked, sounding unsure, which was unlike her.

"It's perfect," Laurel promised.

Kenzie scrunched her lips. "Would you tell me if it wasn't?"

Maybe she should have brought Saffron or Callie. They would have matter-of-factly told her if she looked terrible, if she was an old woman trying to pull off a color reserved for little girls.

"Kenzie," Laurel admonished as if she couldn't believe Kenzie thought she would lie to her. "This, I would be brutally honest about. I know how much this dress means to you. I told you to your face that the yellow organza was simply the worst, remember?"

Kenzie laughed. That was the truth. She almost hadn't shown it to Laurel because it was so bad, but then she'd decided it was so bad she *had* to show it to Laurel. They'd both gotten a great laugh.

"You look like you are ready to get remarried," Laurel said with a smile.

"I do, don't I?" Kenzie turned to take in her reflection in the three mirrors that showed three different angles of the dress. She loved each one. It was a chiffon wrap dress with sheer long sleeves that cinched in at the wrists. There was a tasteful slit up to her lower thigh and the sash was just a shade lighter than the rest of the dress, slimming her waistline. The V-neck was deep but not boobage-falling-out deep. It really was the perfect dress. Even the color, one Kenzie would have never considered had she not seen the dress, was perfect.

"Well, then let's get it," Kenzie said with confidence when she'd had her fill of gazing at her own reflection. She headed back to her dressing room to change and returned moments later, dress slung over her arm. She even loved the feel of the chiffon against her skin.

"Any fun plans for the evening?" Kenzie asked as she led Laurel to the register where the salesperson was waiting with a hopeful smile. She'd been helpful in finding this exact dress for Kenzie and had to be excited about not only helping Kenzie find her dress but the commission that would surely be coming her way.

"I'm thinking about driving into the city to meet up with the kids for dinner. It's their weekly sibling dinner night and it's Mari's turn to cook, so the food should be halfway decent," Laurel said, followed by an almost imperceptible sigh.

She was probably imagining that drive, Kenzie mused. It wasn't as bad on a Saturday evening but still wasn't great. Especially alone.

But she also knew Laurel didn't really want to spend the evening alone at her place. Saturday nights got pretty rowdy in her neighborhood and best-case scenario, it would be loud until the wee hours of the morning. Worst case, the cops would be involved.

"Bryan and I are just doing a night in. You could always join us," Kenzie offered as the salesgirl rang her up. She handed over her credit card, her attention fixed on Laurel.

Laurel eyed her friend skeptically. "Um, no. But thanks. I think I'd rather take my chances with my neighbor's rottweilers."

Kenzie laughed. She didn't blame Laurel. She would hate third wheeling it as well.

"You know you could have a date if you wanted one," Kenzie teased as she thanked the salesperson and left the store.

When Laurel didn't respond, Kenzie glanced at Laurel and saw her gazing down the street toward Riley's office. Longingly.

That did it.

Kenzie hadn't pushed her because she thought it was too soon after Laurel's divorce, and Laurel hadn't seemed completely interested in Riley earlier. But that look said otherwise.

Without a word she looped her arm through Laurel's and walked her right past their cars.

"Hey, where are we going?"

"I happen to know that the man you're thinking of is a complete workaholic because he has yet to find a woman who makes him want to go home," Kenzie said, marching briskly and dragging a startled Laurel along.

"Who, what, why?" Laurel asked in rapid succession.

"You are smart enough to know those first two answers. Why? Because he's a great man and you want him. So go get him, Laurel." Kenzie was a little out of breath by this time but didn't slow down. Riley's office hadn't looked this far away when she started speedwalking.

But they were only about a block away now. Just steps from Laurel's future.

"Kenz, I can't. He probably didn't mean what he said." Laurel tried to free herself, a look of panic on her face, but to no avail. Kenzie had at least twenty pounds and half a dozen inches on her tiny friend, and she was unashamedly using it to her advantage.

"Riley doesn't say things he doesn't mean. He's a man who knows what he wants and goes after it. And what he wants is you, dear friend," Kenzie replied with a grin.

"What if I don't want him?"

Kenzie scoffed but stopped in her tracks when she saw the mixture of terror, hope, and uncertainty on Laurel's face.

"Okay." She turned to Laurel, putting her hands on her petite friend's shoulders. "Say it."

Laurel pursed her lips and looked everywhere but at Kenzie.

"I want him," she finally whispered.

"Aha!" Kenzie proclaimed triumphantly.

"This is so scary," Laurel protested as Kenzie began pulling her again.

"But think about the reward."

"This isn't like me."

"You told me just yesterday you want to push your boundaries."

"This isn't pushing them. This is obliterating them!"

"Po-ta-to, po-tat-o." Kenzie panted now. Laurel was really digging in her heels but she wanted this. Kenzie knew she did.

"Wait!" Laurel gasped when they got to the front of Riley's office. Her whole body was trembling.

Kenzie halted.

"What am I supposed to say?" Laurel asked.

"Besides 'I'm madly in love with you'?"

"Kenzie," Laurel said, the warning strong in her tone.

"How about, 'I am ardently and madly in love with you'?" Kenzie amended.

"Pretty sure that didn't work out too well for Darcy."

"True. How about, 'You know that date you offered, big boy? I'm ready to take you up on it,'" Kenzie said confidently, adding a simper for effect.

Laurel shook her head. "That's too Sandy at the end of *Grease*," she said, crossing her arms uncomfortably.

"Who do you want to be?" Kenzie asked.

"How about 'Laurel who's really scared to tell the guy she's liked for longer than she's ready to admit that she likes him'?" Laurel said tentatively, biting her lip.

"Oh, I like that one. They live happily ever after," Kenzie replied.

Laurel grinned.

"But I don't think I write the line in that one," Kenzie added quietly.

Laurel nodded and took a deep breath, still chewing her poor lip.

A sudden movement caused Kenzie to look up. The door to Riley's office was opening and the man himself was walking right toward them.

"Ready or not, it's showtime," Kenzie muttered, suddenly feeling nervous as well.

"Ladies," Riley said, joining their impromptu party on the sidewalk.

"Riley," Kenzie responded with a smile.

Laurel was silent so Kenzie gave her a helpful nudge.

"Hey," Laurel squeaked before closing her eyes.

Kenzie imagined there was some kind of pep talk happening in her head or maybe a berating. Or even a combination of both.

"It's a beautiful Saturday, isn't it?" Riley asked, though Laurel's eyes were still closed.

"Mm-hm," Laurel managed. She opened her eyes and squinted in the sun.

Kenzie had no idea what to do. Leave. Stay. Leave and sneak behind a car so that she could eavesdrop.

She'd either be doing option two or three, that was for sure. But poor Laurel had turned mute again, so Kenzie would stay by her side as long as she was needed, to be her cheerleader. Or coach, as the case may be.

"We were just talking about how Laurel has no plans for tonight," Kenzie said and then cringed.

Okay, that wasn't her best work.

Laurel's glare said that she thought the same.

"Oh yeah?" Riley asked, grinning.

He knew why they were there. Hopefully Laurel saw that, and hopefully she also saw how thrilled he was to see her.

"Yeah. I thought I'd see if you were free. Since you were

saying maybe we should go out sometime?" Laurel asked. Her voice was shaky but audible.

Kenzie began to back away. Laurel had this.

"I believe my words were more along the lines of 'Watch out, because I'll be asking you out soon.' I should have known you'd beat me to it," Riley said with a smirk.

Kenzie watched her friend nearly melt. Riley's smirk was pretty danged cute.

And with that, Kenzie knew her work was done. Riley really was one of the best guys she knew. He'd treat her sweet friend well. And if not, well, he'd have four Rosebud girls to answer to.

CHAPTER EIGHT

SAFFRON DROVE up the unpaved drive that led to the Lodge, trying to sort through all the things on her mind. No, that was a lie. Just one thing, front and center. All the time, ever since he'd quit four days before. She was angry and frustrated, but mostly just sad that Alex no longer worked with her. She'd been way less tense in the kitchen whenever he was around. Partly it was because she knew he'd have her back no matter what, but also he knew just how to joke if she was having a bad day or if she was worried about something or . . . Alex just got her.

And what was worse was that as long as Cherry was around, Saffron couldn't even be friends with Alex anymore. Not that they'd been friends for very long before Cherry, but she still felt a keen loss. Her life felt emptier now, as if she had a hole she couldn't fill. She hadn't been exaggerating when she'd told her friends she didn't want to talk about Alex. It was too painful. It was ridiculous how much she missed him, considering all he should be to her was an ex sous chef.

But now that she'd had four days of reflection she could finally be completely honest with herself. Alex had been way,

way more than just a coworker. Saffron's feelings had developed to a point where it was probably a good thing he no longer worked for her. It wouldn't have been right, especially since he had a girlfriend. Saffron was head over heels for Alex. He'd found his way into her heart and she couldn't kick him out.

Agh! She was a fool.

Saffron barely refrained from banging her head against her headrest before turning off her engine and opening the door.

The late spring air hit her nose before she even exited the car. Suddenly she was a little less melancholy. Not happy by any means, but hopefully her grouchiness had subsided a little. For the sake of her kitchen staff, if nothing else.

She gathered her purse and to-go mug of coffee and was just about to stand when she felt a shadow fall across her.

Her heartrate picked up to an unhealthy pace and she was just about to throw her still-hot coffee on whoever was behind that shadow when he spoke.

"You're a hard person to track down," Alex said. His voice didn't do anything to lessen Saffron's racing heartrate.

What was he doing here?

Saffron stared straight ahead, but she could still see Alex's sure stance out of the corner of her eye. Her whole body felt his commanding presence.

Dang, she'd even missed his posture.

"Well, I'm here now," she said, hoping her voice sounded way less affected than she felt.

"You are. But only because I cornered you. Why aren't you answering my calls?" Accusation laced Alex's tone.

Whoa, whoa, whoa. Who was accusing who here? He was the one who'd quit and left her high and dry. He was the one who'd let Cherry dictate his life to such an extreme that Saffron was no longer even allowed to be friends with his mom. If they were going to start throwing around accusations, Saffron had plenty to toss into the ring.

"I'm sorry. I didn't realize I had to keep my phone line open for former employees."

"You've been ignoring my calls."

"I didn't know you'd been calling." Saffron told the truth.

"How?" Alex scoffed as if he didn't believe her.

"I deleted your contact from my phone. My phone ignores all calls that aren't from my contact list," Saffron explained. At the look on Alex's face she kind of wished she hadn't. How was she going to explain deleting his number? That wasn't what a boss typically did when someone quit their job. But she'd needed to do it for her own peace of mind, or she would have been the one calling Alex incessantly, trying to figure out why he'd quit. She'd had to break that connection.

"Why?" Alex asked the question Saffron had been dreading. What could she say?

"I didn't see the point in keeping it," she finally said. It was brief. To the point. Maybe a little vague. But it worked.

"And you also didn't see the point in going home?" Alex asked.

Saffron whipped around, looking at him through narrowed eyes. "How do you know that?"

"When you wouldn't answer my calls I had to see you. But you didn't come home for the past two nights," Alex said sheepishly.

Yeah, he should be sheepish. That practically bordered on stalking. But she guessed she could understand. She would have been pissed enough to stalk Alex if he hadn't been answering her calls.

"I've been staying at my brother's. They're out of town until next week and needed someone to hang out with their dogs," Saffron explained.

Alex let out a huge sigh of relief.

"What was that about?" Saffron asked, gesturing at the sigh that seemed to linger. She was still a little annoyed. Maybe she should have answered Alex's calls, but he still didn't have a right to be upset with her right now. That was her place.

"I just . . . I was just worried that maybe you were seeing someone," Alex said softly.

Why would Alex be worried that she was seeing someone? As if that was any of his business, considering he'd left and Cherry and . . .

"With how protective Nick has been of you, I couldn't help but wonder," Alex added.

"Nick? As in the guy who works in our—I mean, *my*—kitchen, Nick?" Saffron couldn't help her laughter. The idea was preposterous.

"What? He's a good-looking man."

"Yeah? Then maybe you can date him," Saffron said through her laughter. "The kid is like fourteen."

"He's twenty-nine."

"Yeah, a baby." Saffron was now hiccupping from laughing so hard.

"It's just that he's barred me from the kitchen for four days straight. It seemed like he was protecting you from me, and not just for professional reasons, you know?" Alex said as Saffron's laughing calmed.

What had he just said?

"You've been here?" Saffron asked.

"Every day since you fired me," Alex responded.

"Since you quit," Saffron amended.

"I wanted to finish out my two weeks. You kicked me out of your kitchen."

"Your girlfriend caused a scene in my kitchen and then you

wanted me to keep you around for two more weeks? It made sense for you to leave immediately."

"It made sense for you to listen to me for two seconds."

Saffron huffed. They were going nowhere. As much as she ached to continue this conversation because she wasn't sure when she'd see Alex again, her feelings for Alex were still so strong that she needed to walk away. She was already imagining things like thinking Alex was worried she was seeing someone. She must have misunderstood him. No way was she going to sit here and keep misunderstanding things until she said something stupid.

He was seeing another woman. How much clearer could it be that he wasn't interested in Saffron?

"I need to get to work," Saffron said, standing. Her body was nearly flush with Alex's because he was so close to her car.

She needed to move. They were too close. She was way too distracted by how tall he was, the perfect height to counter her five-foot-nine frame.

She had to look up a few inches to gaze into his eyes.

What the crap was she doing?

She not-so-gently pushed at Alex's arm since he wasn't moving an inch. Hadn't she just said she needed to get to work? Why had she touched his arm? She was a sucker for a muscular frame, and holy moly did Alex possess that frame.

"Saffron." He folded those muscular arms, making them bulge even more. "I'm not moving until you hear me out."

Fine. Whatever. He didn't have to move. He was close, but not so close that she couldn't sidestep him. The last thing she needed was for this conversation to continue. She needed to be done. It was time to move on, to leave Alex behind. Or ahead, since he finally had the job he'd been dreaming of. And she was happy for him. Alex deserved his own kitchen in town so he didn't have to move away from his mom. He also deserved a woman who adored him, and it seemed like Cherry fit the bill even if she was a little unhinged.

He was happy. Saffron would be happy for him . . . from a distance. Until she could squash those pesky feelings that couldn't seem to take a hint.

Saffron managed to sidestep Alex but when she tried to close her door, he was in the way. They were in a safe neighborhood, but no place in Northern California was safe enough to leave a car door standing open all day.

"Please move, Alex," Saffron said, although the words were more like pleading by the time they escaped her mouth.

"I will. After you hear me out."

What choice did she have?

"Fine," Saffron huffed, crossing her own arms now and taking a purposeful step back. She might have to hear Alex out but she was going to do it in her own space, away from his muscles and intoxicating cologne. She couldn't quite escape his gorgeous face, but that would be gone soon enough. As soon as he said his piece and she escaped to her kitchen.

"I was hoping there would be a little less steam coming from your ears when I told you this," Alex began.

"This is as good as it's going to get." Saffron wasn't in the mood for teasing or playing games. Spending this much time with him was weakening her resolve. All the time she'd spent building a wall around her feelings for him, and it was crumbling in just a few moments of hearing his voice. She couldn't let it collapse completely. Not until he was long gone.

"The scene you talked about in your kitchen with Cherry?"

He was not keeping her out here just to talk about his relationship.

Saffron turned on her heel. She could buy a new car if that one got stolen because she left the door open. She had relatively good insurance. She couldn't remember at the moment if they covered theft, nor did she care. She was leaving.

"She's my ex-girlfriend. That's why she was so mad," Alex said to her back.

Saffron paused. Had he just said . . . ? But then again, breaking up with Cherry meant nothing to Saffron. He could have done it because he wanted to be single again. Or because he was into some other woman.

But why was he telling Saffron if that was the case? Why did he seek her out?

"I broke up with her about a month ago," Alex said.

Saffron spun back to look at him. Had he said a *month*?

"Working for you was torture," Alex continued.

Now where were they going? Was he trying to tell her what a bad boss she was? Saffron was losing her ever-loving mind.

"But I told myself just being your friend was enough. I knew you'd never date a coworker."

Oh. Saffron went completely still.

"And then you started hanging out with my mom. You fit so well into our home, my life. But we couldn't be more. Not while you were my boss. I couldn't quit working at the Lodge, though. It was my only option with my mom sick and no other job openings in town. I felt trapped in my own feelings; I was going crazy. So I did the only thing that seemed to make sense. I tried to transfer them to someone else."

"Cherry," Saffron said quietly.

Alex nodded. "I was a terrible boyfriend. I threw myself into the relationship with her to try to forget you and not only did it not work—I couldn't ever get you out of my head—it made Cherry think I was way more committed to her than I actually was. So when she started asking things of me I had to give in. It was only fair after putting her through this sham of a relationship."

Saffron drew in a deep breath. She'd had no idea. Her hands felt shaky and her chest was tight. This was a lot.

She thought Alex was trying to say that he shouldn't have dated Cherry because he was into her, but she wasn't completely sure. A small part of her was screaming that of course that was what Alex had said—hadn't she heard a word coming out of his mouth? But Saffron had silenced that part of herself for so long she couldn't trust it. Besides, her brain felt like putty, so couldn't she have totally imagined his words? Or read too much meaning into them? She needed Alex to be completely clear, starting with the timeline.

"So you got the job and then broke up with her?" Saffron asked bluntly. It seemed a little harsh. But then again, staying with a woman Alex didn't really want to date was probably worse. Breaking things off might have been best for both of them.

Alex shook his head. "I broke up with her three weeks before Mario offered me the job. I knew it wasn't fair to either of us. She didn't take it well, though. I tried to ease into things by saying we could stay friends."

Wait, what was Alex saying? Saffron couldn't keep up. It sounded like something she'd hoped he'd say for months now, but it couldn't be right. Was she completely misunderstanding? Was her love-addled mind sending her all the wrong messages? She couldn't afford to believe he was saying he had feelings for her if that wasn't true, if he didn't spell it out plainly.

"I've been searching for a job almost since I started in your kitchen. Don't get me wrong, there isn't a chef I'd rather work with. But I wanted so much more with you," Alex said.

She wished he wouldn't be so cryptic. So much more? More what? Baking cakes along with the other food they cooked together?

"When Mario said their head chef was moving on, I

jumped at the chance. I'd broken up with Cherry, and now I had a new job. Nothing was standing between me and the woman I truly wanted. The one I'd wanted for over thirty years."

Nope. That couldn't be her. Was he telling this story about some other woman? Saffron was about to lose it. She had to hear him say it.

"Who?" Saffron asked, hopeful yet dreading the response.

"Who?" Alex parroted, tilting his head in confusion.

"Who do you want? Who have you known and liked for over thirty years?" Saffron pressed.

Alex laughed, but Saffron didn't join him. She was closer to crying than laughing.

"Alex," she pled. Her heart couldn't take the suspense any longer.

"You aren't joking?"

Saffron shook her head.

"You. Always you, Saffron," Alex said. His voice rang with so much sincerity she couldn't deny it. Even her love-addled mind couldn't have misunderstood that.

"Really?" she whispered.

"Really," Alex stated as he started to close the distance between them. Saffron could once again smell his incredible musky scent.

"But thirty years?"

"You knew I had a crush on you back in high school," he said.

"A little one."

"A massive one. And then you left town for thirty years."

"I was working."

"And thankfully so busy working you forgot to date."

"I dated." Saffron defended her workaholic past.

"Hey, that wasn't an accusation. That was all gratitude. I'm so grateful we're here right now. That you didn't date so I can still shoot my shot."

Of course he had to use a basketball metaphor. Thankfully it was simple enough that Saffron understood it.

"But we were finally back in the same town together, and I realized that you hated me," Alex remembered.

"I didn't hate you," Saffron tried to lie.

"I'm sure the word 'nemesis' was uttered."

Okay, he wasn't wrong.

"And I slowly won you over," Alex added.

He had.

"Only to realize I couldn't date my boss."

"Yeah, that would've been messy," Saffron agreed. Her voice was breathy as she watched Alex move closer and closer.

"But now we're here. You don't have a boyfriend," he said.

Saffron shook her head as Alex's strong arms enveloped her waist.

"I don't have a girlfriend," Alex continued.

Saffron trembled as he drew her in closer.

"And you aren't my boss anymore," he finished.

"Maybe I shouldn't have deleted your number," Saffron said lamely.

"Nah, I'm pretty glad we're having this conversation in person," Alex said with a grin.

Saffron had to admit she was glad too.

She could feel her heart pound against her chest and wondered if Alex could hear it.

But instead of giving into the same fear she'd had for too long, she lifted her head, opening herself up to Alex.

Ever the smart man, Alex seized the opportunity immediately, closing the distance between them as his warm, soft lips met Saffron's. The crushing kiss was far from calm, and in it Saffron felt Alex's fierce longing mix with hers. The kiss quickly became heady, and she was sure she was about to fly away. The pain of the last weeks receded, replaced by intense joy that was all the sweeter for the misery she'd endured.

"Fin-al-ly!" Saffron heard Callie call from behind her. Judging by the claps and cheers they had quite the audience.

But Saffron couldn't bring herself to care. She was kissing the man she'd been dreaming about for months. Maybe her whole life. And she wasn't about to stop now.

She looped her arms around Alex's neck, trying to pull him closer. Maybe she'd never stop.

CHAPTER NINE

"SO THIS IS the way we end?" Wells said. With a backpack over his shoulder he looked nothing like the country music superstar he was. He looked like a friend, a father, maybe even an ex-husband—the kind of down-to-earth man Hazel had first fallen in love with.

"Pretty sure you all ended over a year ago when those divorce papers were signed," Sterling teased before giving his dad a farewell hug.

Both boys would be staying with Hazel until the end of the summer, when Chase would go back to Tennessee to attend Vanderbilt. To say Hazel and Wells were proud of their son for getting into such an incredible school would be the understatement of the year. That news had been one of the brightest spots of Hazel's cancer journey.

"Hey, answer my FaceTime calls," Wells admonished his younger son.

"Hey, how about not calling while I'm in school? You got my phone confiscated," Sterling sassed back.

"You got your phone confiscated since you forgot to turn off your ringer," Hazel defended Wells but then turned on him.

"But yeah, you really should remember the hours the boys are in school and not bug them then."

Sterling pulled away from his dad, a smile on his face. They knew they'd be seeing one another soon. School would end in a few weeks and Sterling wanted to spend a good portion of his summer break back in the town where he grew up. After some time away, he was beginning to realize there were things he really did love about Nashville, things he actually missed. Hazel had also overheard Chase advising his brother that a trip to Nashville over the summer was sure to get the attention of the girl Sterling had been crushing on for the past few months.

Chase gave his dad a quick hug as well and then the boys escaped, Sterling to the basement where his video game was paused and Chase to the kitchen to somehow eat once again.

"Wells, I—" Hazel began.

"If you're going to gush about how amazing an ex-husband I am and that you're coming to regret your decision of divorcing me, I've got to stop you there. I love you, Hazel. Always have, always will. But we are better off this way," Wells said.

Hazel laughed at his pure audacity. That speech sounded a little familiar. Maybe because it was the same one she'd given to him.

"You are a goof and as annoying as all get out. But you are the best ex-husband in the world and I can't thank you enough for stepping up these past few months. I know putting your life and career on hold hasn't been easy and . . . " Hazel threw her arms around her ex and he immediately returned the hug.

"It was good for Nashville to lose me for a minute. Now they're chomping at the bit for me to return and no one will dare mention that there are younger, rising stars that can take my place. No one can or will ever take my place."

"Now there's that ego I know and love," Hazel murmured as she continued to hug Wells. There was a certain comfort in the familiarity of a hug she'd felt innumerable times over the course of two decades.

"If Dylan messes up," Wells began.

"He won't," Hazel interjected.

"But if he does? I know people," Wells said, lifting an eyebrow meaningfully.

Hazel pulled out of their hug, grateful Wells didn't say anything about waiting in the wings for her. She wanted him to be happy. And she knew for a fact that he would be happier with someone who wasn't her.

"Pretty sure I know the same people," Hazel said with a shrug. She had been married to the man for twenty years, after all. Most of their friends and acquaintances were shared.

"Yeah, but they like me more," Wells said with a grin.

"They probably do." Hazel didn't doubt it. Wells wasn't just a star thanks to his deep, croony voice. He had the charisma to control and awe an entire stadium. Everyone loved Wells . . . except for Dylan.

"And don't start working so much that the only women you date are your groupies," Hazel added.

"I don't have groupies. They're called Wells Worshippers," Wells corrected.

Hazel cringed. "Somehow that's worse."

Wells lifted a shoulder in defeat. Even he heard how bad it sounded.

"But I'll do it. I'll date a nice girl I can introduce to you and my mama," he promised.

"But you know Mama will still hate her," Hazel said. Her mother-in-law had been all too happy when Wells had become all hers again. She'd tried her best to hide it, but her personal belief was that no one was good enough for her baby boy.

"You'd be surprised. Mom doesn't hate every woman I date."

"Just the good ones?" Hazel joked. Kind of. So far she had been the best thing to ever happen to Wells. Even if they didn't work well together, she was still better than all of his other girlfriends combined.

"Just the best ones," Wells corrected, squeezing Hazel one last time.

"Love you, Haze," he added and then dropped his arms, stepping back.

It felt like a momentous occasion. He wasn't just literally stepping away, but was metaphorically moving back, giving Hazel her space to move on. To be free of their past, free of him. Free for Dylan.

"Love you, Wells," Hazel responded, tears pooling in her eyes. Despite all of the bad days, there had been so very many good ones. Wells was one of the best men she knew, and she was grateful for their time together. It had made her the woman she was.

"And if you ever get cancer, I'll put my life on hold to come hire you a cleaning lady, get meals delivered, and halfway parent our sons," Hazel joked. She had to add some levity because the moment was getting too serious. She and Wells didn't do serious.

"See that you do. And I'd prefer a cleaning lady about half the age of the one you have here. Brunette, about five-foot-six," Wells joked right back.

"Got it. Old, blonde, and super tall or super short. I think I can do that," Hazel said with a wink.

"Are you sure you don't want me to drive you to the airport?" she offered again.

"That's what car services are for," Wells said just as said car pulled into Hazel's driveway.

A man like Wells couldn't just use an app to order a car like the rest of the world. His agent had arranged some super private company to send a driver for Wells. Superstars couldn't take ubers.

"I'll call the boys every other day," Wells promised.

"You'll annoy them if you call that often."

"I know," Wells grinned. "And I'll be calling you daily, darlin'."

"Don't you dare."

"Preferably when you're on dates."

"Wells," Hazel warned but he ignored her, offering his bags to the driver who had joined them at the front door.

"Tell Dylan I said hi," Wells said with a pump of his eyebrows. Then he jogged after his driver and disappeared into the sleek black car.

Hazel waved from her front porch until the car turned the corner and then stepped back into her home, closing the door behind her.

She heard the tv in the living room; the sounds of monologue drifted toward her. She knew Sterling was in the basement. And yet the house felt a little emptier. As annoying as the man was, she was going to miss baseball games blaring at all times of day and night. She was going to miss his excuses that his dishes had to be left in the sink because what would the cleaning lady do with herself if Wells did all the cleaning before she got there? But most of all she'd miss his big presence. The comfort he'd brought for the last six months. That man who drove her up the wall had given her so many moments of comfort and peace during the scariest months of her life.

Hazel blinked away her tears. It was silly to cry. Wells would surely keep his promise of calling daily and she'd soon be cursing his name. He would be in her life forever, thanks to their boys. This wasn't a goodbye.

And yet it was the close of a chapter, a time she'd once thought would never end. She had a feeling Wells would find that right woman for him sooner rather than later and Hazel would no longer be the most important woman in his life. It was the way it should be, considering he was already no longer the most important man in hers. But it was bittersweet, as endings often were.

Hazel's phone buzzed in her pocket. If this was Wells . . .

But when she pulled it out and saw Dylan's name on her screen, her heart lifted and stomach flipped just at the thought of the man who now held her heart.

With Wells it had been goodbye, but it was right. Goodbyes made room for hellos.

"Hello," Hazel said, holding the phone to her ear as an involuntary smile spread across her face.

"I've been waiting all day to hear that hello," Dylan said his deep voice, instantly soothing her even as it excited her.

Yeah. Hazel had been waiting to say it, too.

CHAPTER TEN

A KNOCK on Laurel's door set off her "security" system. The barking—doubled, thanks to the *two* rottweilers her neighbor owned—gave her an immediate headache.

"Rufus! Brutus!" Laurel yelled, even though she knew it wouldn't change anything. She hadn't actually met the dogs; she'd only overheard her neighbor yell those names. But she was really hoping against hope that miraculously the dogs would listen to her this time. She knew Riley was on the other side of the door, and she'd really hoped her neighborhood would put up a good showing. Okay, maybe that was asking a bit much of her neighborhood, which, as Laurel graciously put it, was eclectic. If gunshots at three am, cop cars at four, and Rufus and Brutus around the clock could be called eclectic.

At least the gunshots had been a one-time occurrence. Or so Laurel told herself. She would be living here for the foreseeable future, since it was all she could afford while trying to repay the people her ex had stolen from, so she wanted to make the best of it.

Flustered from the barking and thoughts of gunshots, Laurel smoothed down the skirt of her blue dress, dotted with cute yellow flowers. When Mari had heard Laurel was going on a date, she'd insisted on lending a dress since she knew her mother's closet had been downsized to nearly nothing after the divorce. And although Mari's clothing was adorable and tasteful, most of it was perfect for a twenty-something, not for the fifty-something Laurel. Mari had insisted Laurel didn't look her age and could pull off any look, but the last thing Laurel wanted to do on a first date with a man like Riley was to appear as something she wasn't. But then they'd found this tiered midi-dress in the back of Mari's closet, something she'd bought but had never worn because it made her look like a mom, and Laurel knew it was the one. Even though she looked like a mom, she now looked like a cute and trendy mom ready to go on a date with the town's most sought-after bachelor.

Ugh. She was going to be sick.

She drew in a deep breath and told herself it would all be okay. Even if he was the dream man of every single woman in the town, he was just Riley, her friend and confidant through her divorce and all that had followed. He was the man who'd stood by her side when many others had failed her. He was the one who'd made her smile when it felt like her world was falling apart.

A sense of calm filled Laurel as Riley knocked a second time. She really needed to answer that before he was completely deaf from the barking.

"Hi," Laurel said, sounding breathless as she opened her front door.

She wasn't sure if her breathlessness was due to yelling at the dogs, the gorgeous man standing on her doorstep, or the fact that she was just plain nervous as heck. She hadn't been on a date in years and if the three hours she took to get ready were any indication of how rusty she was, she wasn't sure how this day would go. Truth be told, she hoped it would go really, really well. She truly liked Riley, judging by the number of hopes she'd pinned on this date.

"Hey," Riley said, his appreciative gaze impossible to miss.

How long had it been since a man had looked at her the way Riley was looking at her now? She knew once upon a time Bennie must have gazed at her like that, but probably not in the last ten years. Laurel somehow felt completely content but all stirred up at the same time. What was this man doing to her?

Laurel opened her mouth to start a conversation but at that moment Rufus and Brutus decided to ramp up their barking so she decided it was just better to leave and save the talking for the car. Away from the barking. And the possible gunshots.

They were just a one-time thing, reminded Laurel's inner voice that was trying to help keep her sane. Except if it was just a one-time thing, how had Laurel gotten so unlucky as to experience them in her first week living here? And why did it seem like all of her neighbors hadn't been concerned in the least? When she'd tried to talk to Rufus and Brutus's owner, he'd laughed and walked away while Laurel was still speaking, as if her concern was a joke. Not that the guy was very talkative anyway, Laurel still didn't know his name.

"You look beautiful," Riley nearly yelled as Laurel stepped outside. Somehow the barking sounded even louder out here. Poor Riley.

"Thank you," Laurel said in a normal voice and realized there was no way he could have heard her.

"Thank you!" she practically shouted. Yeah, they really needed to get out of here.

"I was going to bring you some flowers but a little birdie told me that you were more of a chocolate kind of woman," Riley said, presenting a gorgeous, gold-wrapped box of chocolates.

Laurel grinned from ear to ear as she accepted the truffles. They were her absolute favorite and the fact that Riley had done his homework to find out what she would really want meant the world to her. Even after years of marriage with Bennie, he still gave her the things he thought she should want rather than the things she truly desired.

Stop. She needed to quit comparing Riley to Bennie. It was hard since these were the only two men she'd dated in the last thirty years, but it wasn't fair to either of them if she continued. Bennie was Bennie and Riley was Riley. One was in her past and the other . . . well, Laurel hoped he might figure heavily into her future.

Thankfully the box of chocolates was small, so Laurel tucked them into her purse instead of wasting time by going back into her apartment. The sooner they escaped from Rufus and Brutus, the better for everyone.

Laurel took Riley's offered hand and turned her head to hide her goofy grin, biting her lip hard to keep a giddy laugh in. She was holding his hand.

She knew as a mature woman of grown children this shouldn't be the monumental moment it was, but delightful shivers were running up her spine and she had to let them out in some way. She quickly released her lip but the smile was apparently on her face to stay. She couldn't help it. Everything about this moment felt so incredibly delicious. Well, besides Rufus and Brutus.

She hurriedly led Riley toward the stairwell, barking following them all the way. It began to diminish as they hurried down the stairs, but just as they rounded onto the final set of stairs a delightful yet hard-to-swallow part of Laurel's neighborhood appeared.

Oh Heavens, no. She'd somehow forgotten about Monty.

Laurel glanced at Riley, unsure how he would respond to Monty.

Too late to warn him. Laurel pasted a smile on her face as

she greeted the man she saw almost every time she left her apartment.

"Don't look at that car down there, Laurel!" Monty exclaimed as she and Riley made their way down the last of the steps of the apartment building that had seen better days. Even though the stairway was open, the smell of urine was impossible to miss and Laurel didn't even want to know what the green stuff on the rails was.

To be fair, the urine could be thanks to Monty, the homeless man who had taken up residence in front of her building and was often seen sleeping in that stairwell.

Laurel had tried to help Monty find a shelter but he'd told her that he couldn't be contained by "the man." He was born to live right where he was.

Laurel didn't understand how he could feel so passionate about the stairwell and sidewalk in front of her complex, but to each their own. She did try to make sure she had some kind of food to offer him daily, though. The sweet and sometimes slightly off his rocker guy was always willing to take anything Laurel would give him.

"It's a drug deal going down," Monty said in a stage whisper as Laurel and Riley approached him.

Okay, this was definitely not the impression Laurel had wanted to make on Riley, but oh well. The man was here and he was seeing her neighborhood for what it was.

"If we just keep our heads down ain't no one going to care about us, Laurel," Monty said, staring hard in the direction opposite the drug deal.

Honestly, Monty had been a Godsend for Laurel. Who knew how she would have gotten through her first couple of weeks living here had it not been for this slightly crazy man who gave her daily advice.

"Good looking out," Laurel said to Monty as Riley watched the exchange with a blank face.

The man had a great poker face, thanks to his courtroom experience. But Laurel really hoped he'd share what he was thinking. Was this neighborhood too much for him? Would he want her to meet him at other places from now on? Or would he say it was all too much effort—that she was too much effort? Was this date over before it began?

"Yes, thank you," Riley added, calming Laurel's erratic internal questioning.

He wouldn't be thanking Monty unless he meant it, right? And that meant that he wasn't about to leave Laurel behind, didn't it?

Okay, her questioning was continuing. It was just at a less rapid rate.

"Who's this here?" Monty asked, as if suddenly realizing Laurel wasn't alone.

"This is Riley," Laurel said and then added, "And Riley, this is Monty."

"Nice to meet you, Monty. Anyone who's looking out for Laurel is a friend of mine," Riley said, offering his hand.

Laurel's eyes went wide. As sweet as Monty was, the man clearly hadn't washed his hands in some time. Riley was either brave or incredibly kind. Laurel was putting her money on both.

"Oh, sir, I don't shake hands. Germs," Monty explained, stepping back and holding his hands in the air.

Laurel bit her lip to suppress her giggle. Monty was the best.

"Completely understandable." Riley nodded and dropped his hand, somehow managing to keep a completely straight face. The man was a saint.

"I guess we'd better get going. But really, thank you for looking out for Laurel," Riley said with a sincerity that nearly knocked her over. She'd known he was a good man but to speak with such respect to a homeless man that many would count as no one, and then to truly care about Laurel's welfare . . . she felt the sudden urge to kiss him.

But right in front of Monty probably wasn't the place.

Riley placed Laurel's hand in the crook of his arm as he continued to lead her to his car, parked on the street. Thankfully it was in the opposite direction of the drug deal, but a quick glance back showed Laurel that one of the cars had already left. The deal itself was over but one of the participants —Laurel didn't know if it was the buyer or seller—was still parked somewhere behind her and Laurel was grateful to avoid him or her.

Riley opened the passenger door of his Audi. It wasn't the flashy luxury car that Bennie had driven, but it was nice enough to stick out like a sore thumb on Laurel's street. To be honest, Laurel's used Camry stuck out as well. Any car that wasn't lifted or dropped or covered in rust was glaringly different here.

He helped her into the car and after the urine-drenched stairwell, it smelled heavenly. A mix of Riley's bergamot cologne and freshness, like freshly washed laundry.

Laurel sucked in a deep breath as Riley rounded the car to his seat. She wished she could bottle this up and smell it for the rest of her life.

Riley slid into his seat and locked the doors, a smart move on his part, and then turned to Laurel.

She was surprised he wasn't peeling out to escape this neighborhood. Whenever Laurel got in her car, she didn't waste any time sitting there. One never knew what could happen.

"Laurel," Riley said and she felt her stomach drop. This was it. He wasn't moving because he was going to break up with her. Could they break up if they weren't even together? Not really. But he was trying to let her down easily, being his usual considerate self. This visual of just a portion of the baggage in her life was too much for him.

"Don't hate me," he continued.

Laurel wrapped her arms around her stomach. She'd known she liked Riley, but it wasn't until this moment, as everything ended before it began, that she realized just how much she cared about him. She realized she'd already been planning a future with Riley in it. It was silly, considering this was a first date. But to lose him now?

"But we aren't just going to dinner," Riley said.

Wait, what? That was his bad news?

Laurel grinned, not caring what else he would say. He wasn't dumping her.

"I know you don't want to be beholden to anyone, but you can't live here," Riley said. He shook his head, gesturing first toward Rufus and Brutus's apartment and then to the corner where the drug deal had just happened.

"I know you're a strong, independent woman who has endured terrible moments, but this is too much. Even for you. Even with Monty watching your back," Riley added.

Laurel loved that Riley had added Monty to the tiny list of positives about this place instead of to the overwhelming negatives. But she sighed and shrugged.

"It's all I can afford."

How many times had she thought the same thing? That she couldn't endure living here a moment more, but she had to? It was either this or rely on the charity of her friends or kids. She'd done that long enough.

"I think we can work something out," Riley said, causing Laurel to cock her head. What did he mean by that?

"I've been working with Callie," he continued.

Of course he had. Callie hadn't even had to visit to know exactly what Laurel was getting into with this neighborhood.

Her real estate background meant she knew every road in Rosebud and the surrounding areas, and when she'd heard Laurel's new address she'd freaked and begged Laurel to move back in. But that was exactly why Laurel hadn't shared her new address until she'd already moved her stuff out. Laurel wouldn't have put it past her friend to somehow bar Laurel from taking her things.

"We're both worried about you."

Laurel could see that Riley was choosing his words wisely, trying not to offend her, but she should probably let him know she was beyond that. As much as she tried to put up a brave front, she was scared. She hated that she needed to come home and leave only during daylight hours. She hated that she had to rely on dogs who most likely would not come to her aid if she really needed someone. She was already tired of living in fear and she'd only been here a few weeks. How did others manage it their whole lives?

Laurel had decided that once she helped Bennie's victims her next mission would be to help those who wanted to get out of this neighborhood. She'd already lined up a job interview at the Lodge for one of the neighbors down the hall. Sammie had fallen on hard times but said he was good with plants. The Lodge could always use an experienced gardener and he seemed kind and responsible enough. Laurel knew Callie would take the precaution of a background check, as she did with all of their employees, but if Sammie checked out Laurel hoped this new job would help him to get on his feet and out of that building.

"I know. And I hate that I'm worrying you, but I can't see another solution," Laurel said. She wanted Riley to know she was open to suggestions, but she was pretty sure she'd exhausted them all. Short of charity, she would be in that place for the foreseeable future.

Riley grinned and Laurel suddenly felt hope.

"We think we found one," Riley said as he turned on his engine and left Laurel's apartment building behind.

Even just a few streets away from her building the things that Laurel had always associated with Rosebud came into view. Cute bungalows with well-kept yards, kids playing in the streets, an absence of creepy, stinking stairwells. It really was just Laurel's street that was as bad as it was. But it was also why rent was so cheap.

"Are you going to tell me what we're doing?" Laurel asked as Riley drove in silence.

"I thought it would be better if you saw it before I explained," Riley said, a sly smile on his lips.

What was he up to?

Soon he came to a stop in front of a home Laurel knew well. The yard was mowed but overrun with bikes, scooters, and other toys. Having six kids in a home could cause that.

"What are we doing here?" Laurel asked, gazing over the Fields' front yard.

"Callie and I both thought up of tons of different options. I have people who owe me favors and Callie has quite a few as well. Many of them have living options that would work for you," Riley began. Laurel immediately started shaking her head. Nope. She didn't want her friends calling in favors for her.

"Exactly what we thought your reaction would be," Riley said. "But the Fields don't owe us. They owe you."

Laurel scoffed. That wasn't likely. They'd been some of Bennie's victims. If anyone was in debt, Laurel still owed the Fields.

"You not only kept Lisha from getting into legal trouble when she sabotaged the Lodge, but you also singlehandedly funded her first year at MIT," Riley reminded her.

"Because Bennie took the money they had earmarked for that. I didn't help them. I just made things right."

"Exactly. Something you didn't need to do. It was Bennie who fleeced them, not you," Riley countered.

"But I was Bennie's wife at the time . . . "

"I wish you would stop blaming yourself, but yes, I know that's the way you feel. It isn't the way the Fields feel, though. They're pretty sure you hung the moon and stars."

Laurel laughed. That had to be a joke.

"You'd be surprised how many of us in town feel this way," Riley added in a softer voice, as if he too thought that of Laurel.

Surely that couldn't be the case. If anything, Laurel had messed up this town more than she'd helped it. Or at least she'd been married to a man who had done a lot of damage.

"When they heard where you were living, their offer was immediate," Riley said, pointing toward the side of the house. "Back there is a mother-in-law suite. Mrs. Fields' mom was supposed to move in last month but she's decided to stay in Washington for another year or more. So the Fields have a vacant cottage in their backyard."

"They could rent it," Laurel pointed out weakly, but she could tell she was starting to lose this debate.

"Exactly. To you. They wanted to give you the place for free but I told them you'd never accept. Callie knows how much you pay at your place now, so we offered that. And they were more than happy to take it. They hadn't even been planning on renting out the place because they didn't want a stranger living so close to their children, but since it's you, someone they trust, they couldn't be more thrilled."

Laurel felt her hopes rise, but tried to squash them down with her next words. "I'm sure they could get so much more than what I can pay."

"It's not worth it to them. Not if that price comes with a stranger."

"But can't they find someone else they know who can pay more?"

"They've been looking for the past month. No takers," Riley said. He was beaming now. He knew he'd presented a foolproof case. Oh, Laurel did not deserve him.

"Seriously?" she asked when she ran out of arguments. Lawyer that he was, Riley had anticipated every one that she could have come up with, and he'd refuted them all. He'd gone to all of this work—for her.

Riley nodded as he met Laurel's eyes.

"I just can't believe it," Laurel choked. Unable to say another word, she dove across the console and threw her arms around the man who'd made this all happen.

Riley seemed shocked for a split second before his arms made their way around Laurel's waist and pulled her in tight.

"Better tone down your gratitude. If this is the reaction I get for doing what anyone should do for someone they care about, you'd better believe I'll be doing a lot more," he said. He smoothed her hair back and pressed a kiss to Laurel's forehead.

Warmth spread from that precious spot until it filled Laurel's entire being. If this was what it was like to be someone Riley cared about, sign her up. She was sick of pushing away good things, good people, because she felt she didn't deserve them. No, she wasn't perfect. Yes, she'd made mistakes. But even people who'd made mistakes deserved to move on and even move up.

So she was holding onto Riley. Even just minutes ago, back at her apartment complex, if Riley had told her he'd had enough, it would have hurt but she would have been willing to walk away. But no longer. She couldn't. Riley was a man worth fighting for, and she was a woman who deserved to fight for what, and who, mattered to her.

But apparently no fighting would happen, at least for now, because it seemed like Riley wanted her as much as she wanted him.

She grinned and reluctantly pulled out of the hug as she became aware that the stick shift was digging into her leg. She'd give Riley a better hug later.

As Laurel moved back into her seat, Riley pulled a key from his pocket.

"It's all yours," he said, placing it in Laurel's hand.

"Wait, what?"

Riley chuckled at the flabbergasted look on Laurel's face. "We drew up the paperwork and as soon as you sign it, you can move in. Do you want to see your new place?" he offered.

Laurel threw open the door and jumped out of the car.

"I'll take that as a yes," Riley said, still chuckling as he got out of the car way too slowly for Laurel's taste and took her hand again.

The shivers were back and this time they were combined with tremblings of excitement. Laurel was moving out. She honestly didn't care what the inside of this place looked like. She wouldn't have to worry about muggings, drugs, or gunshots here.

Her thoughts were suddenly interrupted by a shrill voice that sounded nothing like Riley.

"Oh my goodness. It's Riley Matthews. Is he on a date with . . . it's Laurel!" an aged voice said from down the sidewalk. Laurel looked over to see Mrs. Randall out for a walk with one of her daughters-in-law.

"Riley!" Mrs. Randall called out, waving her hand in the air as if they hadn't already seen and heard her.

Riley and Laurel turned away from the cottage, waiting for

Mrs. Randall to catch up. Riley waved back as Laurel swallowed back the laughter that threatened. Typically she would hate being put on display like this but right now she was too happy to care about much. And it actually might be kind of nice for Mrs. Randall to see Riley at Laurel's side. If one of the biggest gossips in town saw them on this date maybe she could spread the news. And all of those other women who'd been angling for Riley would back off and leave her man alone.

Laurel's eyes went wide at her own thoughts. Who was this woman in her mind and . . . well, Laurel kind of liked her.

"Is this business or pleasure?" Mrs. Randall said as she approached, waving a hand between Riley and Laurel and speaking in a way only an older woman could. No hellos or pleasantries. The bluntness was astounding.

The younger Mrs. Randall did nothing to rein in her mother-in-law. Not that she could, but she could at least pretend to try or act embarrassed. But she seemed as eager for an answer as her mother-in-law.

Typically Laurel would wait for Riley to answer, but her discovery of her own self-confidence, along with the fact that she didn't want anyone to step in and mess up what was growing between her and Riley, had her speaking up. "Pleasure," she said assuredly and then realized what she'd said.

Pleasure, really? And oh heavens, she'd probably overstepped. This was a first date. Sure, Riley was taking care of so many of her worries and treating her like a queen on said first date but it wasn't like they were in a relationship. Riley had been single for years. Maybe he had commitment issues, or maybe she was pushing him in a direction he didn't want to go. What if after this date they decided to go their separate ways?

"Definitely," Riley agreed with a squeeze of her hand. He was surely able to read the panic on Laurel's face but he just grinned.

"Hm," Mrs. Randall said noncommittally. But then she suddenly nodded. "I like it. If anyone could tame the town's most eligible bachelor, it would be you, Laurel."

Laurel let out the tiniest giggle. But this was too much. Her emotions were all over the place and now Mrs. Randall was giving her approval and . . . what must Riley be thinking about all of this?

"I'm not sure I'm taming him," Laurel said. "It's just a first date." She said the words even while thinking this was anything but. She'd never heard of a first date like this. But if they got into technicalities that was what it was.

"She's definitely taming me, Mrs. Randall," Riley said with a smirk. "Because if I have anything to say about it," he leaned forward as if he were sharing the secret of a lifetime, "I won't be a bachelor for much longer."

Laurel almost asphyxiated on her own spit but that was nothing compared to the open jaw that the younger Mrs. Randall displayed.

The elder just guffawed. "You'll be breaking a ton of hearts, Riley Matthews. But it's nice to see a good man settle with the right woman. That's what I did for Mr. Randall."

She patted Riley's back before she continued her walk, pulling her daughter-in-law with her and reminiscing about Mr. Randall's wild days.

Laurel stood frozen. She'd dared to consider the future a little because she already felt so sure about Riley, but he couldn't already feel the same, could he? He'd probably just said it to get a reaction out of Mrs. Randall.

"Should we go look at the place?" Riley asked calmly, as if he hadn't just rocked her world. He must have just been teasing Mrs. Randall.

"Sure," Laurel said as she followed Riley up the driveway

and to the side of the house where she caught sight of a small white guesthouse with a cute little red door.

"I've always wanted a red door." Laurel tried to concentrate on her possibly new apartment. Her life was changing, she was hopefully moving again, and yet all she could truly think about was Riley's words on repeat.

"I've always wanted to give you what you want," Riley said smoothly.

Too smoothly, right? She couldn't even guess what was serious and what wasn't anymore.

Riley opened the door and Laurel gasped. The place was tiny but that hadn't caused Laurel's reaction. She was utterly smitten with the small cottage. It was already furnished with a table just to her right, the perfect place to leave her purse and keys, and beyond that an inviting cream couch and a pale green rug she could sink her toes into when she sat down. A matching ottoman sat in the center of the living room with a TV tastefully attached to the wall. Just past that was the prettiest little white kitchen Laurel had ever seen. The countertops, cabinets, and island were all white and on the side of the island closest to the living room were four cream-colored barstools that harmonized with the couch. A fiddle-leaf fig on either side of the couch added a homey feel and the stainless steel appliances gleamed.

"There is no way I can possibly afford this," Laurel said. She dropped her eyes, not wanting to see another detail and become further attached.

"They've already agreed. The space is tiny. They couldn't get much more for it even if they did rent it to a stranger."

"I'm sure they could get more."

"They don't want more," Riley replied firmly.

Taking a deep breath, Laurel decided to believe him. She was sick of arguing and she really, really wanted to call this place home.

"So it's mine?" she asked, still struggling to grasp the amazing fact.

Riley smiled when he realized she was giving in.

"Just sign the dotted line." He lifted a stack of papers from the table where Laurel already envisioned setting her things each evening after work. "You can move in tonight."

With tears in her eyes, Laurel threw her arms around Riley again, bathing in the comfort of his embrace. She could honestly stay here forever. How? What? Why was this happening? Those were all real questions, but Laurel decided not to ask them. She was just going to accept the goodness and then look for ways to pass it on.

"I don't deserve you," she murmured into Riley's chest and then realized how that might have sounded.

She pulled away, her embarrassment no longer allowing her to enjoy their hug.

"Not that I have you. I mean you're here, but you're not mine. I mean—" Laurel stopped talking and clapped a hand over her mouth before it could get any worse.

She buried her face into her hands, her cheeks bright red.

Laurel felt a warmth at her wrists as Riley's fingers wrapped around them and gently tugged down so that her face was exposed.

"I meant what I said out there, Laurel. Honestly, I don't know that I would have had the courage to say it to your face, so I'll have to send Mrs. Randall a thank you gift. But I meant it. This might just be a first date, but I've thought about dating you for a long time. Too long. I've wanted you in my life for so many years. I've seen your goodness and tried not to covet you when you were with another man. But now that he's foolishly exited your life, I am not letting any more time go by without telling you what I feel for you. You are the most incredible woman I've ever met, Laurel. And if you would do me the honor, I want to spend every day from this moment with you. I would love for you to be my girlfriend . . . and one day much more," Riley kept his gentle hold on Laurel's wrists as he poured out his heart right there in her new home.

She was trying to register all he was saying. He wanted more too. He felt what she felt. They were somehow in the same spot on this strange road they were traveling.

"I think it's your turn to respond," Riley said. He still had a smile on his face but it was strained, nervous. To think she, Laurel, could make a man like Riley feel that kind of emotion?

She really should say something, though.

"And here I thought you were going to leave me behind at my apartment complex because I was too much for you to handle." Laurel tried to speak lightly but her voice shook slightly. She was still stupefied by Riley's confession. She knew it should be too much for a first date, but Riley was right. They'd had plenty of time for feelings to grow. She could honestly say she'd felt nothing for him while she'd still been married, but after that, he'd been one of the reasons she knew she'd made the right decision in divorcing Bennie. Even as she'd tried to deny everything she'd felt for Riley.

Riley chuckled before tugging Laurel's wrists, pulling her back into his chest.

"And here I thought my confession would be too much for you to handle," he said, his deep voice reverberating through Laurel since her body was flush with his.

"I guess that means we were made for each other," Laurel said. She would have never dared speak these words to anyone other than Riley. But with Riley she knew she was safe. All she did was safe.

"Thank goodness you think so too," Riley said before leaning down and claiming Laurel's lips with his.

Laurel reached up on her tiptoes, more annoyed than ever

with her tiny frame. She needed to be closer to Riley. Her hands reached up to wind behind his head, attempting to tug him down to her level.

And suddenly she was off her feet, Riley lifting her by her waist. Laurel clutched his arms for dear life but was distracted from her shock by the muscles that greeted her hands, tight and strong. Passion swirled in her belly.

A knock at her front door brought both of them back to earth . . . Riley figuratively and Laurel literally. She pushed away from Riley's chest as he carefully set her down. Heavy breathing reminded them of what they'd just done.

"You should probably get that," Riley said, his voice huskier than before. Laurel couldn't believe she'd done that to him.

But if she just stood there staring at him she'd probably jump into his arms again, so she followed his suggestion and opened the door.

There stood the entire Fields family. Laurel was glad the front door didn't have a window of any kind or they would have been giving the young children quite the show.

"So what do you think?" Lisha asked eagerly. "You'll live here, right?"

"What happened to 'no pressure'?" asked Alice, Lisha's mom, as she turned to her daughter with a raised eyebrow.

"I think no pressure went out the window when the entire family decided to show up on the doorstep," Lisha muttered.

Laurel laughed aloud. That was true.

But she was fine with pressure because she knew her answer.

"If you all don't mind, I'll be moving in tomorrow," Laurel said.

The moment the words were out of her mouth, raucous cheers filled her tiny home. Lisha and her siblings were dancing as Alice clapped for joy and her husband smiled.

But it was the reaction behind Laurel that captured her interest the most. Riley put his hand on her waist and whispered into her ear, "Sounds like a plan. Until your next move, that is."

Again Laurel shivered in delight. Would this be a normal thing now that she was Riley's girlfriend? She was Riley's girlfriend! And his words had promised so much more.

Laurel leaned against the man who was making all of her dreams come true and grinned as she watched the Fields family continue to celebrate.

Who would have thought this was where she'd find happiness? After scandal, divorce, and living on her friends' charity, she hadn't imagined she'd be here—next to the man she adored, in a tiny cottage thanks to people Bennie had victimized. Life was funny, but it was good. Oh heavens, was it good.

CHAPTER ELEVEN

"SO ALEX TELLS you he quit his job so that he can date you and the first thing you do is hang out with his mom?" Kenzie raised a skeptical eyebrow nearly to her hairline.

"Raquel, pass me the onions," Saffron said instead of answering her friend.

It was a little rude not to answer her question but then again, Kenzie was the one who'd invaded her space while she was still working, so what did she expect?

Saffron sauteed onions expertly as she whisked her famous cream sauce with her other hand. She'd selected Alex's replacement but the new sous wouldn't be able to start until next week, as she'd had to give two weeks notice to her previous boss. That, coupled with the fact that Nick had to take a few days off for a wedding in San Francisco, meant this wasn't the first time in the past couple of days that Saffron had been cooking two things at the same time.

"Raquel, that needs to go out to table nine immediately," Saffron commanded as she watched one of her other line cooks dish up a plate of linguine.

"On it, Chef," Raquel said with a mock salute, grabbing the plate.

The woman might have some attitude but Saffron didn't mind. Raquel had stepped up big time. Saffron wasn't sure if she would have seen this side of Raquel had things not become so dire, but in crunch time she'd really come through. So much so that Saffron would be leaving at eight pm, after the dinner rush but before they closed, so that she could spend time with Alex's mom. And she'd be leaving Raquel in charge of closing.

She was a little nervous but Raquel had proved herself . . . and Kenzie had promised to keep watch over the kitchen and her sister. It wasn't that Saffron didn't trust Raquel; it was more that she really trusted Kenzie.

"Will you stop talking to my sister and focus on me?" Kenzie demanded loudly, doing everything she could to get Saffron's attention besides physically turning Saffron's face toward her.

"Your sister is actually working. In a kitchen that has six tables waiting for their meals. So yeah, that's the sister I'll be communicating with," Saffron retorted. She sprinkled some white pepper in her cream sauce and it was complete. Now she could just focus on the soup she was prepping for tomorrow's lunch. Because not only did she have to get the meals out for dinner tonight, but Saffron knew if she didn't get a head start on tomorrow they'd be behind before the day even started.

"What I'm talking about is so much more important than a measly meal," Kenzie snapped, her arms flying into the air.

Saffron sighed, passing the cream sauce off to Raquel, and turned to add veggies to her homemade minestrone. The soup sold out every day and Saffron was more than a little proud of that.

"I'm serious, Saff. Alex is completely into you. And it kind of feels like you're brushing him off," Kenzie said, concern etching over her pretty features.

Saffron kept stirring but finally turned her attention to Kenzie. Thankfully this soup was something she could make in her sleep.

"Kenz, I'm not brushing him off. We have a date set up for next week. We've decided to take things slow and it felt like a little time to think before our first date was a good idea," Saffron answered as she added her homemade broth to the soup. That was the secret. She made her own mix of turkey, beef, and chicken bone broth. It did make the dish no longer vegan, but her customers didn't seem to mind. She made a vegan version every Friday, but that one never sold as well.

"You both thought it was a good idea?" Kenzie needed Saffron to clarify.

"Of course," Saffron said, brushing off Kenzie's concern. Alex had agreed to the date being later, so he clearly thought it was a good idea as well, didn't he?

"Why are you keeping him at arm's length, Saff?"

Saffron looked around the kitchen, grateful that her staff was too busy to be paying attention to her conversation. There was plenty of gossip about her and Alex already, especially when all of her employees found out that he'd quit for her.

"I'm going out with him, aren't I?" Saffron asked, feeling more than a little defensive because she *was* keeping Alex at arm's length. But truth be told—not that Saffron would ever tell this truth aloud—she was scared. Alex was a forever kind of guy, the kind Saffron had grown up dreaming about, but she had intentionally never dated those kinds of guys. Life seemed safer when dating was fun and her only commitment was to her family, job, and friends. But when she started dating Alex, she knew things would move in a direction she'd never traversed and that thought scared her to her very core. "And I'm hanging out with his mom," Saffron added.

"What does that have to do with anything?" Kenzie asked.

"Women don't hang out with men they're dating's moms unless they are not brushing off a guy."

"One, I didn't understand a word of that, and two, you are distracting me. Meaning I was right. This date-in-a-week thing is a tactic to keep Alex at bay. Why? Don't you like him?"

Maybe too much, was Saffron's first thought. But what she said aloud was, "Of course I do. We are going on a date." She said the last sentence slowly so that Kenzie could keep up.

"You can plan a date while still avoiding it."

"Now who isn't making sense?" Saffron asked.

"Ugh!" Kenzie put her hands on either side of her head. "Admit it, Saff. You're scared. It's okay to be scared, but you have to admit it."

Saffron let out a loud sigh, putting her soup on simmer, and directed Kenzie to her office. That last outburst had been loud enough to get the attention of everyone in the kitchen.

"Fine, I'm scared," Saffron admitted as soon as she closed the door behind Kenzie. She knew her friend wasn't letting this go.

"Finally," Kenzie said as she sank into Saffron's chair. Count on Kenzie not to sit in the guest chairs.

Saffron leaned against a wall because she honestly didn't feel like sitting down. Not after her admission.

"Of Alex?" Kenzie asked.

Saffron shook her head. The thing she was most sure about in all of this was Alex. Alex was the kind of man she wanted. What she wasn't sure of . . . was herself. How would she cope in a serious relationship, because that was surely where this was going if Saffron gave the green light. Alex had quit his job for her. If that didn't say serious, what did?

"Of myself," Saffron said honestly.

Kenzie pursed her lips so Saffron continued. "Alex really likes me."

"A good thing," Kenzie interrupted.

"It is. A really good thing. But I don't do relationships, Kenz. I am fifty . . . " Saffron muttered her real age. Of course Kenzie knew it but Saffron still didn't like saying it out loud. "And I have somehow managed to stay single, unmarried, all of it, for all those years. If that doesn't tell me I'm good at being single but would mangle a relationship, I don't know what would."

"You don't do relationships with the wrong men. That's a great thing."

Kenzie's words caused Saffron to pause.

"You and Alex have never tried a relationship. What if you are still single for this very moment. For this relationship?" Kenzie asked.

"I know this remarriage stuff is turning you into a romantic, but sometimes the most right answer is the most obvious answer. Maybe I'm not in a relationship because I shouldn't be in a relationship."

"And sometimes the right answer is that you're scared so you're searching for an excuse to prepare yourself for a bad ending when what you're really doing is dooming your relationship before it starts. You could be keeping it from being the most beautiful thing to ever happen to you." Kenzie crossed her arms over her chest in a satisfied manner.

"Okay, I understood most of that. But what if you're wrong?"

"What if I'm right?" Kenzie asked.

Oh dang. What if she was right? Wasn't it worth putting all she could into this relationship, even if it meant a broken heart down the line? Then she'd at least know she'd done all she could.

Saffron was about to give in when she remembered one small detail. Something that still bothered her, and the only reason she'd wondered if Alex was all in.

"And you don't think I should be worried that he dated Cherry up until a few weeks ago?"

"That he had a casual relationship, much like you had tons of casual relationships, but this one grew out of control and the not-so-sane woman thought there was more to it than there was? And he only had said casual relationship to try to forget that he couldn't have you but it didn't work at all because no one matched up to you, so he quit his job to date you even though he wasn't sure of your feelings for him? Absolutely not," Kenzie answered.

Once Saffron registered all Kenzie had said, she realized it was a very good answer. And Saffron knew Kenzie was right. She knew Alex's true feelings for Cherry because he'd told her so. She just hadn't been sure if she wanted to believe him. Not because she didn't trust him—he'd always been truthful with her —but because believing him meant letting go of her one remaining doubt about him. Deep down she wasn't sure she was ready to fully give her heart to whatever this was they were starting.

"You have to let Alex in. You have to, Saff . . . or you have to let him go. You can't just keep him at arm's length. I know your defense has always been to keep a shield up and it has worked out for you. Because none of the guys you've dated in the past have been worth dropping that shield."

"But Alex is," Saffron whispered.

"He is," Kenzie agreed.

"I'm pushing him away."

"You are." Kenzie grinned like she'd just won the Nobel Peace Prize. Honestly, if she could move Saffron into a relation-ship that was actually an even more elusive conquest.

Saffron let her head hit the wall behind her. She'd been so stupid. Would Alex forgive her?

Of course he would. He'd always forgiven her, and heaven knew she'd been just as silly or even more so in the past. Holding onto her grudge against him from high school hadn't been her finest moment.

"So are you going to cancel on his mom and go out with the hunk of a man?"

Saffron laughed as she shook her head. "I can't do that. Paula has been so good to me and I can finally hang out with her again now that Cherry is out of their lives."

"Thank goodness," Kenzie muttered when she heard about Cherry.

Saffron agreed wholeheartedly with that sentiment.

"But after Paula goes to bed—she usually hits the sack pretty early—I'll talk to Alex. I'll tell him I that was afraid but I'm going to push that fear aside. That I'm all in." Saffron drew a shaky breath and set her jaw determinedly. Wasn't a man who was willing to quit his job for her worth that?

He definitely was.

"GOOD NIGHT, MOM," Alex called out, exiting his office just after Paula had walked down the hall to her bedroom.

He'd spent much of the evening in his office. Apparently his new restaurant wanted a menu overhaul now that he was head chef and Alex had been granted his lifelong wish of creating his very own menu. It was a huge amount of work, but Saffron was excited for him. There was nothing like cooking the foods you loved in your very own kitchen.

But Saffron was also very glad that Alex had decided to come out of his menu-planning cave now that his mom was going to bed. She wasn't sure she would have had the nerve to go into his office and start the conversation she'd promised Kenzie she'd have tonight.

"Did you and Mom have fun?" Alex asked as he sank into the couch cushion beside Saffron, lifting his arm and giving Saffron room to nuzzle into his side.

Okay, so this was bliss. Saffron's body warmed the instant it touched Alex's.

"We watched a backlog of about twenty episodes of *Wheel of Fortune*," Saffron said, glad that Paula had been having such a good night. From what she'd heard from Alex, they weren't happening as often as they used to and Saffron was grateful she'd landed on a good one after not seeing her for so long. She figured there would be many bad ones in the future, but this first good one had been a blessing.

She smiled as she remembered that Paula had saved as many episodes as she could on her DVR to watch with Saffron. Paula loved all game shows, but this was her favorite and she'd wanted to watch it with Saffron. That meant the world to her. Paula had started saving episodes while Cherry was still in their lives, hoping Saffron would one day be back. The fact that Paula had done something so sweet . . . Saffron loved that woman.

"And it's safe to say your mother is still the puzzle-solving master," Saffron added.

Alex chuckled. "I've never seen anyone get those answers faster than she does. Did she tell you about the time she was on the show?"

"And how your dad ruined it for her because he kept on spinning bankrupt?" Saffron laughed.

"He didn't ruin it for me," Paula called from down the hall, showing she wasn't quite in bed yet. "It just made it a little difficult to win. But the wheel had it out for us, not my dear husband."

Saffron grinned. Would she one day speak about a man in such reverent tones? Would that be how she felt about Alex?

Because she was well on her way to those feelings, it wasn't hard to imagine. And again, fear shook her. Saffron wasn't the kind of woman to think about a forever kind of relationship. She had always appreciated short timelines. But Kenzie was right. All of the men she'd dated in the past had only deserved short timelines. Alex was the kind of man one gave more to.

Finally, she heard the click of Paula's door shutting. It was time.

"So," Saffron began, her heart beating against her ribcage. It was now or never.

"So," Alex mimicked, pulling Saffron in closer to his side.

This was what she'd been pushing away. These quiet moments of just the two of them. These heart-stopping moments where Saffron wanted nothing more than to press her lips to Alex's. Why the heck was she running from that?

But she was getting ahead of herself. They had to talk. She had to reveal why she'd pushed off their date. And then she had a question for Alex as well. After speaking with Kenzie, she'd thought that all her worries about Cherry were gone, but they were still there. Typically Saffron would keep these kinds of worries to herself; they would either resolve or self-destruct a relationship and Saffron had been fine with the latter option in the past. But not this time. So she had to dive. To be vulnerable.

Ugh. Saffron hated being vulnerable.

She drew in a deep breath, reminding herself she'd worn her big girl pants. She could do this.

"I want to apologize," Saffron began.

"For what?" Alex asked, his eyebrows raised in question.

"You came here and made my mom's night, while giving me a whole evening to work on recipes. You are a gem."

Alex kissed Saffron's forehead, and she swore she felt actual sparks. It would be so easy to just say, 'oh, that's true' and move to the kissing part of the evening, but that wouldn't be right. Saffron had to be honest. If she wanted this to work, she needed to give it her all. After some deep thought she'd realized she desperately wanted this to work.

"Because I wasn't exactly honest with you. I am busy. Super busy. You left me in quite the lurch," she said with a teasing grin.

"I know. And I wish I felt badly about it. But I don't. At all. Because leaving that kitchen means I can do this and you aren't worried about fraternizing with the help." Alex pressed a kiss to her cheek, and Saffron nearly forgot her resolve to have this conversation.

She laughed. It was true.

"No, but in all honesty, I do feel badly that you're working so hard," Alex said before kissing the top of Saffron's shoulder. He really needed to stop this. She only had so much willpower.

"Alex," she said, mustering every part of her strength to pull out of his embrace. She had to say this. "I *am* working a lot. But not so much that I couldn't go out with you sooner. Nick actually gets back a few days before our scheduled date. He could totally take over training the new girl."

Saffron let out a sigh of relief at getting it off her chest until she saw the look of confusion on Alex's face. Oh gosh. She'd bungled that. She needed to explain better.

"I was scared. I am scared. Of this, of us. I can feel we're the real deal and I don't want to mess it up, and yet at the same time I'm so scared of not messing it up right now and then messing it up later when we're both completely involved and head over heels. Because that's where I see myself, Alex. Head over heels. For you. In the not-so-distant future. I've never felt like this."

Saffron expelled another breath and to her relief she saw Alex nodding.

"I didn't think I'd ever feel like this either. I thought that part of wanting forever with someone was broken in me," Alex revealed.

Saffron nodded enthusiastically. That was exactly how she'd felt as well. Everyone around her had been pairing off for years, so she'd followed the pattern. But each time she dated, she hadn't felt passion. If they left, they left. With Alex, everything was different.

"I was scared as well. Still am scared. Why do you think I dated Cherry?" Alex scrubbed a hand over his face.

Oh, thank heavens he'd brought her up. Saffron finally had a sufficient answer to the question she had promised herself she'd ask. And she hadn't even had to be the one to ask Alex about it.

She sighed an even bigger breath of relief. Alex had been scared. It made so much sense. That's why he'd dated Cherry. If anyone could understand doing stupid and irrational things because of fear, it was Saffron. She'd almost missed out on all of this with Alex because of her own fears. She could totally see herself dating a Cherry as well, if it had kept her from facing what she felt for Alex head-on.

"It was a combination of knowing you wouldn't date me while I was your sous but needing the job because I couldn't get another one anywhere near my mom. And then when I thought about actually dating you, an absolutely petrified feeling came over me. You were the woman I'd dreamed about for so long that I measured every other woman against you. Rather than taking that risk, opening myself to the possibility of pain if things didn't work out with us, it was so much easier to let Cherry into my life."

"And let her get her claws into you," Saffron couldn't help but add. It was petty but it was the truth.

Alex chuckled. "Yeah, it felt that way. It was a huge mistake. I led her on and I feel terribly about it."

Saffron nodded, understanding filling her. She and Alex were so alike in so many ridiculous ways. She knew they were going to fight, probably a lot, and they were going to make mistakes, definitely a lot, but wasn't that what loving someone meant? Accepting them, adoring them, even while knowing things weren't going to be perfect?

"We all make mistakes," Saffron said before nuzzling into Alex's side once more. She'd been away from him for too long and needed to feel him against her again. "I'm sure I'll keep making them."

"I will too," Alex added.

"But then we'll talk about them."

"And we'll forgive the other."

"We might fight a bit first."

"We *will* fight a bit first," Alex corrected with a laugh.

"But we'll be honest. We'll come to one another first with our fears."

"And we'll face them together," Alex promised.

Saffron gazed up at the face of the man who had been part of her life for so long and yet she'd never imagined would be right here, with her. At this precipice. She knew if she took this next step there would be no turning back. But after hearing what Alex had to say, feeling how comfortable she was revealing all to him, how safe she'd felt . . . Saffron didn't want to turn back. Alex made her want to jump.

So she would. They would. Together.

"Now it's time for kissing," Saffron said, more for herself than for Alex. She'd been holding off as long as she could. But they'd gotten the hard part out of the way. Now came the fun part.

"Is that so?" Alex grinned as his head tipped toward Saffron. "Then I guess I have to do this." With a last teasing smile he closed the rest of the distance between them.

Yeah he did. And with his kiss came a promise of what was to come. Saffron couldn't wait for all of their future. The fights, the mistakes, the makeups, the comfort, having someone always by her side—and of course, the kisses.

CHAPTER TWELVE

"I'LL NEED a plus one as well," Saffron said as Kenzie asked everyone for a final headcount for her big day. She tried to play it cool but couldn't stop the grin that spread across her face.

All of the girls were gathered in the Lodge office that Kenzie and Callie typically used. Saffron stood near the door while Callie perched on the corner of her desk, having given her desk chair to Hazel. Hazel was nearly as strong as ever but Callie didn't want to push their luck by making her stand when she didn't have to. Laurel leaned her butt against a filing cabinet and Kenzie was holding court from her desk. She'd requested one final meeting before the big day next weekend.

"Seriously?" Kenzie squeaked. "Your talk with Alex the other night went well?"

"I don't like the question in your voice," Saffron responded, narrowing her eyes. "You were the one who pressured me to talk to Alex. If you weren't sure it was going to go well, why did you pressure me?"

"Because I obviously knew it would go well," Kenzie instantly replied, but shot Callie a look of relief.

Callie fought the urge to grin and give away her friend's

secret. All she had to do to keep that smile at bay was to remember she would literally be the only one of them without a plus one for Kenzie's remarriage ceremony.

And she was thrilled for Hazel, that she'd chosen Dylan and the two were blissfully in love. As well as for Kenzie getting her gorgeous second wedding and for Laurel and Riley's kind of nausea-inducing need to be with one another all the time. And especially for Saffron and Alex. For the first time in Saffron's career, she was leaving work early and getting in late, giving more responsibility to her employees so she could sneak in time with her new boyfriend. It was so fun that all of them were acting like fools half their age. Fools in love.

Yet instead of fighting off a smile, Callie was full on frowning. She knew she was being petty. She'd called her friends fools, when the truth was she yearned to be in any of their positions. As long as the man she was with was Leo.

Did she really need to get married?

As she'd helped Kenzie plan her simple ceremony and beautiful but relaxed reception, Callie knew she would be sad to give that all up, to never have that ceremony she'd dreamed of. It was more than just the glitz and glam of it. Dedicating her life to one man in front of God and her family and friends was important to her. She wanted that.

But did she *need* it?

She knew she missed Leo. She felt an ache in her chest each morning when she woke, and she cried herself to sleep every night, even though two weeks had passed. She'd never felt so broken after leaving a man.

So didn't that mean she had to give up the idea of marriage?

She'd gone back and forth, forth and back, always coming to one conclusion. She wanted Leo. She'd give up anything for him. Even a wedding. Even one day being a wife. Even becoming a stepmom to his surely beautiful children. Even if all of that meant taking a step back each time anything happened because she wasn't truly family.

But being willing to do it didn't necessarily mean she wouldn't one day grow to resent Leo.

She couldn't get past that concern. She knew she wanted Leo right now, but if she did end up resenting him, would that break them? Was it better to stay away?

Or could she get completely over the idea of a wedding?

Because that's what she needed to do before she and Leo could have any sort of future together. So she was trying. But it was hard, considering she was helping Kenzie to plan the very thing she was trying to tell herself she didn't need. Some of the details were a headache, but overall planning with Kenz had been a beautiful experience. One she wanted for herself.

And there went her thoughts right back into the hamster wheel that just swirled them round and round.

"Did you all get your dresses?" Kenzie asked, her eyes bouncing from friend to friend.

Kenzie wasn't necessarily having bridesmaids. That would have been too much for her simple day, but she had asked all of her family to dress in sage while the girls were supposed to wear one particular shade of cream. That way they'd have a cohesive look for photos.

Callie nodded and saw her friends doing the same. Callie's dress was beautiful, a maxi with a flowing chiffon skirt and satin top. She'd bought it when she'd still held out hope that she and Leo would have worked through their impasse by this point and had imagined entering the cere-mony on his arm.

Instead she was going to be alone. She guessed the dress would work as well for a single woman as it would for a coupled woman.

But Callie wanted to be a coupled woman. She sighed, realizing she was complaining. And would complaining accomplish anything? No.

But it might make her feel a little better.

As long as she was in this room with all of her friends, though, she was going to keep her mouth shut. And she would smile because this gathering was about Kenzie, not about Callie and her stupid broken heart.

"And we all have rooms reserved for the night before the ceremony?" Kenzie asked her.

Callie tried to grin. This was a happy moment. It was wonderful that Kenzie was getting her second chance with Bryan. They'd worked hard. They deserved it. What they didn't deserve was a friend who felt the need to wallow when they should all be celebrating.

Despite her effort, Callie knew the grin didn't look genuine. Too much of her heart hurt. Better to skip the smile and just answer Kenzie's question.

"I have the honeymoon suite booked for the five of us the night before, but we'll make sure to vacate it so that you and Bryan have it to yourselves after the ceremony," Callie said. She started to suggestively pump her eyebrows but stopped because she doubted she could pull off that look either. "We also have rooms booked for your out-of-town family for the night before and after."

"You're the best," Kenzie said, shooting Callie a grateful look.

Kenzie had tried to unburden her from helping with the remarriage after she and Leo had ended things. But Callie had insisted on doing her part. She wanted to do this for Kenzie. And she was mostly glad she had, except in the moments when her heart really felt like it would break again, knowing she'd never have this with Leo.

"It was nothing." Callie tried to shrug off the compliment.

"It was everything," Kenzie said genuinely.

At that Callie knew she'd done the right thing. Even if it had hurt from time to time.

"So, I think that's it," Kenzie said, beaming at all of them. Callie could only imagine how excited she must feel. She would be walking down the aisle for the second time in her life, but to the same man of her dreams. "I can't believe it's just five days away!"

Callie had to smile at that. She loved seeing the people she loved so completely and utterly happy, even if a certain green-eyed monster tried to convince her otherwise.

"Can't wait," Saffron said before adding, "but I'd better get back to the kitchen."

Kenzie nodded as Saffron ducked out with a quick wave to the others.

"And I'll get on the phone with your wedding planner about that question you had regarding the table setup," Laurel said as she stood and started out of the office.

"Thank you," Kenzie called after her.

"And I'm going to go take a nap. I lead a glamorous life," Hazel quipped as she stood from Callie's chair.

"I don't know. I'd say a middle-of-the-day nap is exactly what we're all fantasizing about," Callie joked.

"I one thousand percent agree," Kenzie added as they watched Hazel make her way across the office.

"Do you want me to walk you to your car?" Callie asked her friend.

"Or I can," Kenzie piped up.

"You guys. Stop. I am done with chemo. I know I'm not cured—I won't be able to declare that for at least five years—but I'm as well as can be, considering. I need you all to stop babying me. My boys do it enough for all of y'all."

Her words were stern but she had a smile on her face as she

spoke. She may have felt slightly frustrated but Callie knew she was mostly grateful for all who cared so much for her. She'd told Callie cancer had been the worst experience of her life, but at the same time she'd gotten to see all her loved ones show up for her, and that had been one of the most incredible experiences.

Callie hadn't thought of it like that until Hazel had spoken the words. But it made sense. Sometimes people had to endure the worst to see the best.

"Fine. Fall on your way to your car. See if I care. I won't even help you up," Kenzie said with a chuckle.

"Exactly. Now you're finally getting it," Hazel said as she walked through the doorway.

"Do you want us to kick you while you're down?" Callie asked.

"Why did you have to take it too far, Call? Of course I don't," Hazel said, sending Callie a wink before she left Kenzie and Callie alone.

They sat in silence for a few moments but Callie could tell her friend had something on her mind. She'd hoped to get Callie alone. And now she had her.

"Are you really okay?" Kenzie finally asked, her exuberance from earlier gone.

Callie tucked a bit of her blonde hair behind her ear, stalling. What should she say? She knew Kenzie must have seen pain on her face or she wouldn't have said anything. But she also didn't want to bring up her own grief when Kenzie should be concentrating on the bliss of all that was happening to her, not Callie's patheticness.

"I will be. I just have to figure things out," Callie said honestly. She did have to figure things out. And she hoped she would be okay.

"You really love him, don't you?" Kenzie asked.

Callie nodded immediately. It was the absolute truth so she

couldn't deny it if she tried. She blinked at the tears that sprang to her eyes.

Kenzie knew what was keeping Leo and Callie apart, and she knew how impossible it seemed to Callie.

"Then I truly believe it will work out. You'll make sure of it," Kenzie said. She seemed to have a lot more faith in Callie than Callie had in herself.

"Kenz," Laurel called down the hall. "Your wedding planner said we could meet her in the garden space to go over the setup issues. She'll be here in five."

"Awesome," Kenzie yelled back to Laurel, standing.

But she turned back to Callie before she left. "If any of this gets to be too much—"

"It won't," Callie interrupted.

"You can't be sure. So if it does, just walk away. I give you full rights, as the bride . . . ish. Can I call myself a bride even though it's a remarriage ceremony?" Kenzie asked, cocking her head.

"I think 'brideish' works perfectly," Callie teased her friend.

Kenzie rolled her eyes but seemed grateful that Callie could joke.

"You'd better get out there," Callie said, making a shooing motion as Kenzie lingered, still looking concerned.

Kenzie finally left the office and Callie was all alone.

It was amazing to have people in her corner but sometimes she needed a moment in her corner to herself. She needed to regroup, to get off her hamster wheel and really figure out what she wanted.

Leo. It always came back to wanting him. But for that to work she had to stop wanting marriage. How did she deprogram an aspiration she'd had for fifty years?

Callie sighed before turning her attention to her computer. She'd have to think about Leo later. She had too many responsibilities to wallow in sadness. She needed to get a buyer's contract drafted for a sale she was facilitating as well as other work for the Lodge. She'd finally found a way to juggle both of her jobs. Too bad the rest of her life wasn't as easy to manage.

"Hey, Callie!" Jenny, their front desk manager called into the office area a few minutes after Callie had finally been able to focus on work. "I think you might need to get out here."

Callie looked up from her computer, wondering what could be such an issue that Jenny would call her out there instead of coming back here to speak to her. If it was an unruly customer, Jenny wouldn't have yelled for Callie's help. Was it an employee issue? Had someone broken something again?

Well, only one way to know.

With yet another sigh, Callie stood and stretched, willing herself the strength to get through whatever this was. Problems at work had never really bothered Callie before, but ever since breaking it off with Leo, dealing with these things sapped her energy. Honestly, she didn't have it in her to truly live her life.

Okay, if that wasn't a sign that she had to try to win Leo back, she didn't know what was. As soon as she dealt with whatever this situation was, she was coming up with a plan. One to get marriage out of her head and heart and Leo back in her arms.

As Callie walked into the reception area, she saw Jenny holding a vase of beautiful pink peonies.

This was what she'd yelled to Callie about? Jenny had gotten flowers.

Yet, something niggled in the back of Callie's mind. Peonies were *her* favorite.

But those couldn't be for her. Who would be sending her flowers?

"They're lovely," Callie said as she walked toward Jenny,

still unsure of why she was there. "Who are they for?" she couldn't help adding.

"You," Jenny answered with an enthusiastic grin, waving her arm toward the lobby beyond the reception desk.

In the middle of the lobby were at least thirty more vases, all full of peonies. Some were white, some pink, some red, and even a few yellow and orange.

Callie gasped as she took the vase from Jenny and slowly rounded the reception desk, staring in shock.

"And more are coming," Jenny said as she pointed toward the front door where a cute woman wearing a smock that read *Rosebud Floral* entered with yet another vase in each hand.

Callie knew these could only be from one man, yet she barely dared to hope.

"There must be hundreds of flowers," she breathed.

The scent was intoxicating. She moved to the middle of what felt like an enchanted garden in the middle of the lobby. They were gorgeous.

"One thousand, to be exact," the woman said as she set the vase down on the edge of what Callie was beginning to think of as her garden.

"A thousand peonies," Callie whispered, tears gathering in her eyes.

Please let them be from Leo. She didn't know who else could have done this, but she was still too afraid to let her heart believe. But if it was him . . . he'd remembered.

Callie dimly noticed the Rosebud Floral employee, along with a few coworkers, bringing in more vases, but she was too overwhelmed to really take in anything other than the beauty of each and every flower.

If she hadn't already loved him, this would have definitely tipped her over the edge.

Back when they'd been dating, she'd watched a few episodes

of her favorite TV show with Leo, including one where the main character received a thousand yellow daisies. Callie had melted with the beauty of the moment but had commented that she'd felt the gesture had been wasted by using daisies. A thousand peonies would have been so much better.

She'd never imagined actually receiving them.

Callie knelt in the middle of her garden, setting the vase she held on the floor beside her. They were all so lovely and her heart was lifting with hope, finally accepting that Leo was behind this. It had to be him, right? No one else would do this for her.

But where was he?

Suddenly she heard the sound of familiar boots treading the Lodge's wooden floors. Callie would know that stride anywhere.

She glanced up and there he was, holding the final floral arrangement.

He was here. For her. With a thousand perfect peonies.

The tears that had threatened were now streaming down her cheeks. Each one was a happy tear. No part of Callie felt as if she were giving up anything. In that moment she knew she would regret nothing if she chose Leo.

She stood and wound her way through her garden. Leo had the presence of mind to set his vase down just in time for Callie to fling herself into his arms. She'd missed him so much.

His delicious scent of cedar with a hint of sawdust filled her nose as she wound her arms around his neck and nuzzled her face into his chest.

"A thousand peonies. You remembered," Callie said into his shirt. Looking up at his face would mean pulling away from Leo and right now the only place she wanted to be was right there against his chest.

"How could I have forgotten? Every memory with you is branded into my mind. These last weeks have been slow torture, replaying each of them, knowing I'd pushed you away." Leo's chest rumbled beneath Callie's cheek as he spoke.

"It was my fault too. I shouldn't have pushed marriage. Being with you is more important than anything else," Callie said truthfully. It had taken her a while to come to that conclusion but now she knew. She'd missed Leo from the moment she'd walked away, but that hadn't helped to resolve the crazy internal struggle she'd been fighting every day since then. Until a few moments before, when she'd sat in the middle of those peonies. She'd felt so light, realizing that the struggle was over. Leo had won today, and she knew that in her heart, he'd always win over all else every day . . . forever.

"Yes, you should have. Marriage is something you've always dreamed about. And it's something I can give you. I knew about two days after our last date that what it came down to was my fears or your dreams. Why would I ever choose to let my fears dictate our lives when I could be fulfilling your dreams instead?"

Callie felt wetness on her cheeks. She was soaking Leo's shirt with her happy tears but she still couldn't bring herself to pull away.

"Two days?" she asked.

"Yup. I'm a fool, but a fool who was quick to see his mistakes. The rest of the time I spent trying to figure out the perfect way to win you back. Because you deserved it, after having to deal with me. And knowing you'll have to deal with me forever."

That sounded like exactly what Callie wanted. She knew it wouldn't be the trial Leo was making it out to be. Getting to be with Leo forever made her the luckiest woman in the world.

"And then I remembered this show. Do you know that when we watched it, I catalogued it in my mind as the perfect proposal for you? So I guess I wasn't as against marriage as I had thought. My subconscious had known that to keep a woman like you in my life, I'd have to get married. I'd *get* to be married. To you. I'd have the privilege of committing my life to you."

"Wait, so you're saying . . . ?" Callie's shock at his words caused her to finally pull back and look into his eyes. He wouldn't joke about this, would he?

"I love you, Callie," Leo said, meeting her gaze. "And loving is more important than feeding my fears. It's more important than my job. It's so important that . . . "

Two teens, a boy and a girl, appeared at Leo's sides. Callie had no idea where they'd come from, she'd been so focused on Leo, but one look at them told her who they were.

Callie stumbled back out of Leo's arms and hastily made some ineffectual swipes at her wet face.

"This is Harper," Leo said, gesturing toward the beautiful young woman on his right. "And this is Andrew." He nodded at the handsome young man on his left.

Never had there been two more gorgeous young people. Granted, they had the most beautiful dad on the planet, so Callie guessed it made sense.

"Nice to meet you," she finally managed, trying not to freak out internally that she was meeting Leo's kids.

Harper was the first to move, throwing her arms around Callie. "I've never seen my dad as happy as he'd been while he was dating you and then as miserable as he was when he messed it up big time," she said as she squeezed Callie tightly.

Callie wrapped her own arms around the loveable, beautiful girl. She'd been so sure Leo's kids would hate her, thinking that was the reason he was keeping her away from them. To be greeted so warmly took her breath away.

"Dad's a protector. He was trying to protect us from the pain of seeing him date a new woman. But we're not dumb. We know that after a divorce people start dating again. And we want Dad to be happy. So there was no need to protect us," Harper said, shooting a glare in her father's direction.

Leo frowned. "Not my finest moment."

"But you should know that though his faults are many, many, maaaaany—" Harper drew it out with a teasing glance at her dad.

"You can move along with whatever you're about to say," Leo grumbled.

Harper laughed. "He's actually a pretty great guy." She gave Callie one last squeeze before letting her go.

Callie had a feeling she and Harper were going to be the best of friends.

Leo nudged his son, who took a shy step forward. "I'm not good with words like Harp, but from what Dad's said you sound pretty cool and chill. And you make him get that goofy smile on his face that Harper gets when she meets the newest guy of her dreams, so you must be who Dad loves. And if Dad loves you, we'll love you one day too," Andrew said in a quiet but deep voice that reminded Callie so much of his father.

Callie gave Andrew a sweet but quick hug, knowing that anything more would probably scare the kid. He smiled gratefully as she let go and she knew she'd made the right move.

She had met Leo's kids. And it had gone well. So many of the barriers keeping them apart had fallen by the wayside. She was pretty sure Leo had been about to propose but she had to let him know that was no longer necessary. Callie didn't need a wedding or even a marriage. She just needed Leo. They'd figure out the rest later.

"Thank you," Callie said, first to Harper and then to Andrew. "You don't know what today has meant to me. Meeting you both . . . " Her stupid eyes welled with even more tears, clogging her throat.

She cleared it and continued, "and being accepted by you

both. It's all I could have ever hoped for. I just need you to know Leo, this is enough. Being included in your family, being loved by you. It's enough. I don't need a wedding or marriage or to be a wife. I just need to be with you. To love you and to love these amazing kiddos of yours."

Leo's eyes sparkled. "Well, that's a shame."

Callie's brows knit in confusion. Wasn't that exactly what Leo had hoped to hear? He'd made the grand gesture, he'd bridged the gap, and now she would close it. He didn't have to make all of the concessions. He didn't have to propose. That was how relationships worked: give and take.

"Because I don't know what I would do with this—" Leo pulled a little blue box from his pocket "—if I didn't do this." He dropped to his knee and opened the box to reveal the most gorgeous ring Callie had ever seen. A giant emerald gleamed in a pavé diamond band.

Callie's eyes went wide as her mouth dropped. Her body began to shake. What was Leo doing?

But no. She couldn't let him do this. Not when he didn't want to.

Callie worked on stilling her trembling as she tried to lift the big man off of his knees, but her futile tugs did nothing to move Leo.

"Callie," he said, his voice warm.

"I mean it. I don't need this. I don't want to make you do something you'll regret," Callie said as she kept fruitlessly trying to yank him to his feet.

Leo grinned. "I know I don't need to. You should know me well enough by now that the only reason I'm doing this is because I want to." He stayed firmly planted on his one knee, gently loosening her fingers that still clutched his arm and clasping them in his strong, calloused hands. "I told you that giving you all of your dreams was more important than any of my fears, Callie. You are beautiful, bright, kind, loyal—everything I could dream of in a woman and more. You made me realize that my fears were unfounded, that being married wasn't what I wanted before only because I wasn't married to you. But imagining every morning waking up with you by my side, diving into every problem together, celebrating every joy together, being a stepmom to my children, sharing our grandchildren . . . it wasn't until I almost lost you that I realized your dream was my dream too. Being married to anyone else would be hell. But to you, it would be a dream come true." Leo released one of her hands and held up the ring again. As if Callie had needed anything other than those words to say yes. But the ring was stunning.

"So?" Harper asked. "You ready to be a stepmom to the best kids on this planet?"

Callie giggled. She couldn't believe it. She was still in shock. But she had to say something. She had to say yes!

"Yes!" she shouted and then jumped at the sound of her own voice.

Cheers erupted from around the lobby and Callie realized they'd drawn quite the crowd. She heard Kenzie's distinct whoop and knew her other friends must be around as well.

Leo fitted the ring on Callie's finger and leaped to his feet exuberantly. With a yelp of joy he gathered Callie into his arms and twirled her before setting her on her feet and pulling her in even more tightly. She closed her eyes to breathe in the moment: the weight of the ring on her finger, the heady scent of the peonies, and most of all the strong, warm arms that held her so firmly but tenderly.

"Are you sure you won't regret this?" Callie whispered as she leaned against his shirt, still damp from her tears. It was a beautiful, grand gesture, but did Leo really understand what he was giving up?

"What I regret is every stupid word I said to you at the drive-in. I was an imbecile. How could I have worried that my kids would do anything but love you? How could I have worried about spending my life with you when the worst thing would be a future without you? No, Callie. I will never regret making you mine forever. I had weeks to ponder and I want to voice sacred vows to you that will change everything in our relationship. Promises that will unify us more, help us to understand how sacred the very nature of us being us really is. Marriage will change us. It will take work. I'll be an imbecile again and again, and you'll have to forgive me. But you will, and I'll try to be better. And at the end of the day, we'll love one another fiercely. Our marriage will only strengthen that."

Callie's face hurt from how big her smile was, but she couldn't help it.

"You gave me a thousand peonies," she said again.

"I had to be sure you would say yes. Life without you is pure misery," Leo whispered into her hair.

Callie laughed because she felt exactly the same.

"And one bonus of a wedding I'd seemed to have forgotten," Leo added, surreptitiously glancing around to make sure his kids couldn't hear. "A honeymoon," he added in a low voice as he dropped his head. Callie reached up to meet him, that single kiss lighting her on fire in a way no other could.

"Get a room," Andrew groaned.

"Oh, I plan to," Leo murmured.

Callie giggled.

Who would have thought when she started the day that this was how she'd be ending it? Things weren't perfect, but she and Leo were finally on the same page. They'd chosen each other. He was sacrificing this time and she'd sacrifice the next. It wouldn't be equal, it wouldn't be easy, but it would be completely worth it.

CHAPTER THIRTEEN

CALLIE WASN'T sure how they'd all ended up here, but here they were. The five of them, standing against that fence where they'd first imagined all of their high school daydreams coming true. In a way, it felt like they had.

The Lodge was theirs. It was thriving. In fact, the *Rosebud Gazette* had just run a feature on it, calling it a town treasure. Not only were the residents of Rosebud proud of the Lodge, but guests from all over the world were seeking out reservations in their quaint vineyard-surrounded Lodge. And Callie knew the praise was well deserved. It was a beautiful, unique place.

Glancing down, she couldn't help but watch the way the sun made her ring shine. She'd had it on her finger for a few days now and still couldn't get over how pretty it was. Even more, she could hardly believe that Leo wanted to marry her. Ahh!

But they'd decided—well, mostly Callie had decided—that they would have a year-long engagement. She wanted to give Leo plenty of time to back out if a wedding wasn't really what he wanted. Leo had said there wasn't a chance in hell that would happen. Of course, that declaration had made Callie glow.

She'd been worried that the next morning she'd wake up and Leo would have changed his mind, but so far so good. In fact, during the ceremony today, Leo had held her hand tightly and whispered that he couldn't wait for their turn pledging their lives to each other.

"Did you ever find out why Bryan insisted on calling today a remarriage instead of a vow renewal?" Saffron asked as she leaned against the fence, gazing toward the Lodge like the rest of them.

Kenzie wore the beautiful blush gown she'd chosen with Laurel and the rest of them were in their cream ensembles, looking a little worse for the wear. The ceremony had begun at noon and at the reception immediately following the girls had lived it up. So by now their dresses were wrinkled, and there may have been a few smudges from all the dancing and feasting.

"Yeah," Kenzie said softly, watching the setting sun that glowed behind the Lodge. It really was majestic at this time of day. "We, especially I, even though Bryan won't accuse me, lost sight of what was important back in the city. My focus was on my job, bettering myself—basically anything but our marriage. So after our separation and therapy he wanted to do this ceremony and party as a fresh start, but he also wanted our focus to be on what happens after. Because the renewal of vows and a reception are fun and all but he wanted to keep calling it a re*marriage* because the marriage is his focus. He's hoping it will be mine, too."

Callie smiled at her friend. It was funny how they were kind of at the same place even though they'd taken vastly different roads to get there.

"Aw," Laurel said sweetly. She stood with the others but carefully kept a little distance from the fence. Callie mentally corrected her observation that they all looked rumpled after hours of partying. Laurel still looked like she'd just finished getting ready.

"That's so sweet," Hazel agreed. She was probably leaning the most heavily on the fence. She'd been able to dance and socialize with the rest of the partygoers most of the time. Her strength hadn't fully returned, but the fact that she was still at the party, hours later, showed just how much she'd improved over this past month since chemo had ended. It probably helped that Dylan watched out so carefully for her, hovering nearby in case she needed a helping hand or even just someone to lean on.

Kenzie eyed Hazel with suspicion.

"What?" Hazel asked as Kenzie leaned in closer.

"Something happened," Kenzie said matter-of-factly.

"What do you mean 'something happened'? Could she be any more vague?" Hazel looked to Callie for help, but now that Kenzie had mentioned it there was something suspicious about Hazel. She always got this look in her eye when she was hiding something. This was the downside to having friends who'd known you basically your entire life: they knew your tells.

"What did you do?" Callie pushed.

Kenzie grinned as Hazel's defensive act changed to a guilty look.

"I didn't want to tell you today," Hazel protested. "Today is about you."

Kenzie shrugged. "Pretty sure the 'me' part of the day is over. Now lets make it about the secret you're keeping from us."

"It's not exactly a secret . . . " Hazel was stalling, her cheeks flushing.

"Out with it," Saffron commanded.

Hazel put a hand to her neck, pulling a delicate gold chain from inside her dress. At the end of the chain dangled a giant diamond ring. She unclasped the necklace, took the ring off the chain, and slipped it onto the fourth finger of her left hand. Laurel let out a shriek and basically jumped onto Hazel to hug her before remembering her friend's physical condition and attempting to restrain herself.

"You too?" Callie squeaked as she pulled Hazel's hand close to investigate the gorgeous ring. It was a princess-cut diamond— Hazel couldn't have worn any other style—on a gold band full of pavé diamonds. Perfection.

"Me too," Hazel said with a grin.

"When, what, how?!" Kenzie yelped with joy but also accusation as she swooped in for her hug as well.

"Last night," Hazel began.

"And you kept it from us all day?" Saffron asked with wide eyes, tugging Hazel away from Kenzie so that she could embrace her too.

"It was Kenzie's day," Hazel insisted.

"Next time tell us immediately," Kenzie admonished.

"I seem to recall you hiding your ring when Bryan reproposed and you didn't want to attract attention at my end-of-chemo party," Hazel reminded her. With a shy smile she added, "I don't plan on there ever being a next time." Her smile grew, as if she too couldn't believe that she was settling down with one man again, believing that this was it for both of them. They were choosing one another forever. Just a year ago, Hazel would have never believed this of herself.

But what a difference a year made. Hazel had battled and beaten cancer. Callie knew she wouldn't be officially cured for years yet, but in her mind the battle had been won. Hazel had come out victorious. She had also allowed Wells back into her life and they were friends again, coparenting with the best of them. Most importantly, she'd found a man who loved her, flaws and all, who'd fallen for her while she'd been frail and bald. Hazel had always counted on her beauty, but even without it,

Dylan had stayed completely smitten. Callie couldn't wish for a better man for her friend.

Callie put her arms around Hazel and held on tightly—well, as tightly as she dared. There had been too many moments this year she had worried whether she'd be mourning the loss of Hazel. To have her here, making plans for her future, was inspiring.

"It'll be your turn soon," Hazel told Laurel over Callie's shoulder.

Callie pulled out of the hug to watch Laurel's reaction. The red on her cheeks said it all even as she stammered, "I don't know about that. We're just getting to know one another . . ."

"You've known Riley since high school," Kenzie said with a smirk.

"You know what I mean," Laurel replied.

"Oh, you're getting to *know* him," Saffron teased.

Laurel's cheeks deepened to a shade so bright, Callie worried her friend would combust.

"Leave Laurel alone. Besides, you could be next instead." Callie sent Saffron a pointed gaze.

"I hope I am," Saffron said unexpectedly.

Kenzie's mouth dropped open. "Really?"

"Alex is it. I've dated enough frogs to know I've found my prince," Saffron replied.

"Finally," Hazel squealed.

"Right?" Saffron agreed.

Callie looked around at her friends. Not only had their dream of the Lodge been realized, but another dream, one they hadn't even all dared to dream, had come true. They were all happy, figuring out their careers and life plans and building new lives with men they truly loved. Seriously, what a difference a year made.

"Can you believe we're all here with dates?" Hazel asked, her thoughts apparently along the same lines as Callie's.

"Right? And we actually like them," Saffron added with a smirk.

They all laughed.

"Well, I'm not sure I like your date, yet. He was my friend's archnemesis in high school," Callie teased Saffron.

"Ugh. Do you know that he brings that up almost daily?" Saffron leaned her arms against the fence.

"I don't blame him. You were ridiculous to hold onto that grudge thirty years later!" Kenzie pointed out.

Saffron couldn't say anything because Kenzie wasn't wrong.

"But as surprising as it is that you and Alex got together," Kenzie said, "I think our sweet Laurel has surprised us the most, snagging the town's most eligible bachelor."

"I did get pretty lucky," Laurel said with a soft smile.

"Oh, no. I didn't mean that. He's the one who lucked out for sure. It's just that I didn't see you being able to let go of all of the Bennie stuff and taking charge of your own happiness, at least not yet. I'm proud of you, Laurel." Kenzie stepped close to give Laurel a side hug.

"Yeah, I wasn't sure I'd be able to either," Laurel agreed. Then her eyes narrowed. "But the idea of Riley with someone else?"

Kenzie gasped to hear her meek friend sound so territorial. Hazel threw back her head with laughter. Saffron just shook her head as if she couldn't believe it.

"One of my favorite things about Riley is that he found you a new place. A safe place to live," Callie said.

The others murmured in agreement. They'd all been trying to get Laurel to move, and they'd forever be grateful to Riley for making it happen.

"He's kind of perfect," Laurel admitted shyly.

"Well, then maybe he's almost worthy of you," Kenzie decided as the others nodded.

"Why does this feel like an end of sorts?" Saffron asked as she looked from one friend to another. The sun was getting so low that the light was fading quickly and Callie couldn't quite make out the expression on her friend's face.

"Because when we stood here last time and this was all just a dream, I think we felt that if we ever got to the other side of it, it would be the end," Callie said, pointing up at the Lodge.

"But it's just the beginning, huh?" Hazel said.

Callie totally agreed with her. Honestly, Hazel probably needed the new beginning most of all.

"I hope so," Laurel said optimistically.

"I know it is for me," Kenzie said with a fond glance back toward the white tent where all of their significant others were still enjoying the party.

A bonus the girls hadn't foreseen was that all of the men in their lives seemed to like each other.

"Me too," Callie said as her eyes were drawn down to her ring again. It was just so darn pretty.

"You're right," Saffron said before adding, "but it is also an end. We're closing the chapter where the Lodge was just a dream. Where I hated Alex."

The women laughed.

"Where Callie was married to her job and Kenzie, well, you were married to your job too even though you had a husband waiting at home," Saffron continued and the women laughed harder. "A chapter where Laurel sat in her husband's shadow and Hazel was a bitter divorcée."

"Hey!" Hazel seemed to be the only one who didn't agree with Saffron's assessment.

"Okay, hot bitter divorcée," Saffron amended.

"Better," Hazel said with a small clap of approval.

The friends laughed once again.

Callie was sure her stomach was going to hurt from all the laughter of this beautiful day.

"What do you think the next chapter will bring?" Laurel asked Saffron as if she could see the future.

"A couple of weddings," Saffron answered, nodding to Callie and Hazel.

"Hopefully a few more," Hazel said, gazing meaningfully at Saffron and Laurel.

"Maybe a couple of grandkids?" Laurel added hopefully.

Hazel shook her head. "Oh, no way. I am so not ready for that chapter. That can come about five chapters down the road."

Callie grinned. She loved that Hazel envisioned herself living a long life—so long that she could put things off a bit.

"That all sounds nice, but do you want to know what I know?" Callie asked as she pulled Kenzie in on one side and Laurel on the other. Hazel leaned against Kenzie and Laurel put her arm around Saffron's waist. "No matter the chapter in my life, you all will be there."

She met the eyes of each of her friends in the waning light. She swore she saw tears welling up in a few of them. She knew she felt some in her own eyes.

Kenzie nodded and Laurel smiled. "Can I hear a 'hell yeah'?" Saffron asked.

"Hell yeah!" they all agreed.

They held one another until the daylight had completely faded, the lights of the Lodge and the tent glowing against the night sky.

"Are you guys still out there?" Dylan called.

Hazel laughed. "We'll be back in a moment."

"I thought they'd abandoned us." Riley's voice drifted toward them, letting Callie know that the guys were on their way.

The women shifted positions as their men joined them. Hazel rested heavily on Dylan, showing that she was more tired than she'd let on but was comfortable allowing Dylan to see her need for him.

They stood like that for a few moments, the guys seeming to realize the girls weren't ready to end their time together.

But then Callie met Hazel's eyes and suddenly started giggling. Hazel joined in, followed by the other three in quick succession.

"Not sure what's going on here, but I think it's time we get back to our guests," Bryan said to Kenzie who nodded up at him with a goofy, loving smile on her face.

They led the way back to the party. Dylan followed soon after, with Hazel leaning on him, probably to find a comfortable seat for her. Then Saffron mentioned something about checking on Alex's mom and the two of them wandered back to the tent.

The two remaining couples watched as Saffron and Alex walked hand in hand, Callie snuggled next to Leo's side and Laurel looking just as content next to Riley.

"I think I'm going to love this next chapter," Laurel with a wink at Callie.

Callie reveled in the feel of Leo's strong arm around her, knowing she had the best of friends, and that the beautiful Lodge in the distance was all theirs. She was sure more problems lurked on the horizon but right now she couldn't bring herself to care. Life was good. This moment was perfect. And like Laurel, she was sure she was going to love the next chapter as well.

THANK you for reading the final chapter of the Rosebud series! These women have been such a blessing in my life and I hope they are in yours as well. It is always bittersweet, for me, when I end a series. I usually don't want to do it, trying to figure out ways to keep my favorite stories going. But I knew this was the end for these girls. At least on these pages. In my mind they live on, leading happy and healthy lives, always showing up for one another.

If you haven't had a chance to read Julia Clemens's Whisling Island series, start with *Sunset on Whisling Island* !

Want to stay up-to-date on all things Julia Clemens and know when she's releasing more books? Join Julia Clemens's newsletter here.

Thank you, thank you! And I love you all!!

Made in United States
Orlando, FL
17 February 2024

43811971R00098